Millionaire
Mistress 3

Also by Tiphani Montgomery

The Millionaire Mistress

Still a Mistress

Published by Kensington Publishing Corp.

Millionaire Mistress 3

Tiphani Montgomery

Kensington Publishing Corp.

http://www.kensingtonbooks.com

DAFINA BOOKS are published by

Kensington Publishing Corp.
119 West 40th Street
New York, NY 10018

All Kensington Titles, Imprints, and Distributed Lines
are available at special quantity discounts for bulk pur-
chases for sales promotions, premiums, fund-raising,
and educational or institutional use. Special book ex-
cerpts or customized printings can also be created to fit
specific needs. For details, write or phone the office of
the Kensington special sales manager: Kensington Publishing Corp., 119 West 40th Street, New York, NY
10018, attn: Special Sales Department, Phone: 1-800-
221-2647.

Dafina and the Dafina logo Reg. U.S. Pat. & TM Off.

ISBN-13: 978-0-7582-6327-8
ISBN-10: 0-7582-6327-9

First Kensington mass market printing: April 2012

10 9 8 7 6 5 4 3 2 1

Printed in the United States of America

Millionaire Mistress 3

1

Chloe

Fucked up.
Broken.
Left for dead.
But a bad bitch never died. Not before her time. Not when there were more backs to stab and people to kill. It had been six months since that horrible night in the warehouse where everyone left me for dead. Six torturous months, and my body still hadn't completely healed from the war wounds I received that night. Six long months, and this hospital was the place I still called home, without any money or the love of my life, Brooklyn, by my side.

Yesterday marked my fifth and last surgery to correct the stomach and small intestinal damage that Bella's bullets were responsible for. Those were the same bullets that were meant to end my life. Bella, just nine years old now, had an enemy for life. The pain that the surgery caused would last only for a few more days, but I just couldn't wait for all of this to be over with.

I had places to go.

People to take off the face of this earth.

And money to make.

For six long months, I had remained weak and restless on this piece of shit they called a hospital bed, while I plotted my revenge. I reached over and grabbed the large mirror with the red handle that sat on the food tray. Even though it sat right next to my bed, it took minutes for me to hold it up to my face. Out of fear. Fear of what I would see. Countless times a day, I looked at myself in the mirror, still unsure why I expected to see a different reflection.

It had been only a week since I'd received plastic surgery on my face, and it was still all bandaged up. I looked like a mummy now. But looking like this was much better than the face I had been left with. From the knife that had been dug into the right side of my face, to my left ear, which had been cut off, and not to mention the burns . . . I'd looked like the Elephant Man.

I'd let my hair grow to the middle of my back in an attempt to hide the deformity of being earless, but I wished I had something to cover up my horrible burns just as easily. When Brooklyn left the warehouse, his attempt to set the place on fire succeeded, but he failed at the most important task of getting rid of me. I managed to get out with third-degree burns to my hands, arms, and a small portion of my face. Deep down in my heart I knew that Brooklyn wanted me to live and just had to put on a show for Oshyn. I couldn't wait for the chance to show him that his plan had worked.

I spent every second of every day, every hour of every week, and every month just thinking about how I was going to get each of those muthafuckas back for leaving me scarred for life. Bella, Oshyn, and Mye had to die a slow, painful, agonizing death, but Brooklyn would be mine.

I knew he would.

Even though I relived our reunion daily, this day was different. It was the Fourth of July, Oshyn's birthday. I'd make sure she would never see another one again. I set the mirror on my bed and picked up the hospital phone, placing a call to the only place where dudes got things done.

Rochester, New York.

I had my homey Tuff looking into Oshyn's and Brooklyn's whereabouts, and I needed to know if there was any progress in the search.

It had been several weeks since he'd started his hood search, and my patience had run its course.

He answered.

On the last ring.

Knew it was me. Wanted me to wait.

"Tuff, why do you insist on making me so damn angry?"

Little did he know that me being angry was the last thing he needed.

"Angry? Nobody gives a fuck about your crazy ass being angry. Fuck you, Chloe! And didn't I tell you that I would call you when I got the information?"

I took a deep breath and weighed my options, which included cursing him out, but quickly realized that wouldn't do me any good. I wasn't in a position to make too many demands, so for now I had to comply. Later, I vowed to myself, he would pay.

"Well, when the fuck will you know?" I asked anxiously.

This was as nice as I could be.

"All I know for now is that they're living in another country."

In another country, I silently repeated to myself as I wondered where they could've moved to. Ever since Oshyn heard the horror story of her mother going into labor on a cruise ship, she had never really trusted foreign travel and always wanted to stay in the States, just in case things went wrong. But I could never fully understand why . . . especially since these were all lies.

Her mother wasn't really her mother, and the stories Roslyn made up were concocted only to cushion the blow of the truth of how Oshyn was conceived, which was by rape. I couldn't help but laugh as I thought of how meaningless Oshyn was even at the beginning of her life. Conceived out of hate, she was never wanted. But killed out of hate would be my job.

"When will you know?" I asked Tuff again in my deep, kick-ass voice.

"I just haven't pinpointed where they are yet. I should know by next week, at the latest."

"Next week? Muthafucka, we ain't working on black people time! I need this information now!" I had tried being nice to his faggot ass, but dudes like him only understood being talked down to. He didn't deserve respect. "I knew that your whack ass couldn't get something like this done."

His breathing pattern shortened.

Yet got heavier.

I could sense that I was pissing him off, and I was pleased at how easy it was to throw him off track. He was a man that hadn't mastered his emotions, and I knew that I would be able to take him off his game at the drop of a dime. *This is going to be too easy,* I thought.

"Never send an incompetent little fucking boy to do a grown man's job!" Disgust filled my voice.

His breathing pattern now resembled an asthmatic's wheezing. I was sure that I had struck a nerve.

"Yo, you lucky you not in front of me right now, or I would—"

"Or you would what?" I butted in, not allowing him to finish his sentence. "Kill me?" I laughed.

Hard.

It took all the strength that I had in me to calm myself down. I couldn't remember there ever being a time when I just sat back and allowed a man to talk to me any kind of way and didn't put him in his place at that very moment. But I realized that things had to be handled very differently this time around. If I wanted to win this war, I had to lay siege very carefully with patience and precision. Two of the very things I knew nothing about. Two of the very things I'd had to learn quickly while in recovery.

"Like I said, bitch," he continued, unfazed by my laughter, "you lucky." He paused for a few seconds. "Here's a phone number," he said nastily before rattling off thirteen long numbers. "Try that for now, but I want an extra two hundred if it works."

"Yeah . . . whatever, nigga. Just call me when your dumb ass got my information!"

I hung up on him before my malicious words took control and I ruined everything. Butterflies flew around in my stomach, and my mouth began to water, because I knew that the time was near. I could taste it. By this time next week I would get my revenge. Bandages or not, I'd be on the first thing smoking when Tuff called me with their location.

2

Oshyn

"Happy birthday to you, happy birthday to you, happy birthday, dear Oshyn . . . happy birthday to you!"

Rich.

Dark.

Pecan.

That was the color of my kitchen table, which I sat at, with a smile painted on my face. Brooklyn and Bella serenaded me with the "Happy Birthday" song, while Mye Storie, oblivious as to what was taking place, just smiled and slobbered, seemingly hypnotized by the flames of the twenty-six red, white, and blue candles. The sweet smell of my homemade buttermilk strawberry flag cake made all their mouths water as they waited anxiously for me to blow them out.

"Make a wish!" Bella demanded.

However, I just sat there in the midst of what seemed like hundreds of balloons.

Frozen.

Unable to dream of a better life, one in which my whole family was alive and together again. A life in which my aunt Mahogany and my mother shared sisterly love. A life in which Chloe and I did the same. A life in which my firstborn son and my best friend were back and alive again. And my grandmother's heart didn't fail her because of all the pain this family had caused her.

I just sat there.

Not knowing what to wish for.

Not quite knowing if wishes still came true.

"Hello? Earth to Mother. Is anybody home?" Bella asked sarcastically.

She was grown as hell to be almost ten and insisted on calling me her mom. Even though her fair skin, which was decorated with freckles, and her green eyes both made her look like the spitting image of her mom, Apples, I could tell that she was slowly forgetting who her mother was. I did everything in my power to make her remember, but it was as if she didn't want to. I had concluded that maybe it just hurt too much. Maybe she wanted to pretend as if the last two years of her life never existed. As we all did. As I desperately tried to do constantly.

"Mom!" she said in slow motion.

Her neon green fingernails swayed in front of my face as if she were trying to get the attention of a handicapped person. As if I needed special communication. She straightened the dumb crystal tiara that I was forced to wear back onto the center of my head, and then stood in front of me with her hands crossed over her chest. A chest that had grown breasts the size of mosquito bites. I expected her period to come within a year or so, which was another problem that I could seriously do without.

I felt my husband staring at me as he sat off to the side, holding our son on his lap. I guess he couldn't take any more of my nonresponsiveness when he asked, "Baby, we're waiting on you to make a wish. What's wrong?"

I lowered my head as I felt the tears heading to the surface. I kept my long, silky black hair in the way, because it acted as a curtain that, for the moment, hid my soul. I couldn't answer Brooklyn, either.

So I sat in the kitchen of our large four-bedroom, two-and-a-half-bathroom villa, inhaling the scent of smoked barbecue, cake, and ocean water. The true scents of Independence Day, minus the fireworks, since we no longer lived in the land of the brave.

Saint-Tropez was now the place I called home. Located in southern France, on the French Riviera, my new home was known best for its famous and wealthy guests. The weather

11

was what you would expect of a Mediterranean climate: scorching hot summer days, relieved by refreshing evening breezes, and an incredibly mild winter. There was no place I'd rather be, and I often kicked myself for not thinking about moving here sooner.

I eventually broke out of my trance and looked up slowly like Oprah Winfrey's character Ms. Sophia did at the dinner table before she made her big speech. I had no idea who didn't like the movie *The Color Purple*. It was my favorite.

"Umm . . . ," was all I could muster up before the phone rang for the third time today.

Brooklyn looked at the phone and then back at me and said, "Just forget it. Finish what you were saying."

"No . . . answer it," I suggested, wiping my tears away. I was no longer in the mood to make my big speech. There was something more important that needed to be taken care of.

"Baby, it's probably just my job calling. J'eun was supposed to cover for me today, but he never showed up. This is a holiday. You know the Fourth is the busiest time of the year. They probably just want me to come in because he didn't." Brooklyn turned his back to me. Probably didn't want me to see him lie to my face. "I'm not going in today, so they can forget it," he declared just before the phone stopped ringing.

Chateau de la Messardiere, one of Saint-

Tropez's most popular resorts, was where Brooklyn worked as a bartender. Although it sounded like he made meager wages, we lived more than comfortably in a three-hundred-and-twenty-thousand-dollar home that had great ocean views. The resort was a hot draw for celebrities, models, and moguls, not to mention July being the island's busiest month, but I wasn't buying it.

"No, that's not it," I said calmly. I flung my hair back behind my ears to get the strands out of my face. I wanted him to watch my face wrinkle up, showing him that I meant business. "Two times today that phone has rung, and both times all I heard was someone breathing on the other end before hanging up."

I knew in my heart that something wasn't right, but he was doing everything in his power to convince me otherwise.

The phone rang again.

And then again.

And then again.

And then it stopped.

"There, the ringing finally stopped. Now, please blow out those candles before the wax melts into the cake and we can't eat it!" Brooklyn said impatiently as his six-foot-four frame towered in front of me.

He handed his son, who was the spitting image of him, to Bella and then turned his attention back to me, lowering himself to be able to place his lips on my forehead and then again on my lips.

"Ewww, get a room," Bella snarled as she turned away, trying to avoid the torture of witnessing true love at its finest.

I looked into his gray eyes and suddenly remembered the first time we fell in love, when the worries of the world hadn't yet been placed on our shoulders. Before he betrayed my trust, and I forgave him for his sins.

He brought me back to the present moment as he smiled at me like he always did, showing off his trademark gap, which made me crumble. The wife beater that he had on revealed a body that he'd worked so hard at perfecting, and the tattoos on his arm still read BROOKLYN'S OSHYN and RIP MICAH.

The phone rang again, snapping me from my thoughts of our past, and I found myself staring at Brooklyn, no longer in admiration, but in anger. Telling him through my eyes that he better pick up the phone this time. Thank God he listened.

"Hello? Hello?" He paused and then let his eyes meet mine. "Hello!" he said once more before hanging up.

"Guess that wasn't your job, after all, was it?"

I was being funny, but no one was in a laughing mood. My birthday had been ruined by the anonymous serial caller. I wasn't sure why he didn't want to admit that something more sinister was happening, but I knew.

"Bella, take Mye upstairs," Brooklyn instructed.

"But what about the cake?" Bella whined.

"What did I say?"

His tone got hard.

Fatherly.

"What's wrong with you?" she screamed at me angrily. "We're finally a normal family again! Why are you ruining everything?"

Brooklyn, not believing that Bella had disregarded his instruction and was now talking recklessly to me, lowered his eyebrows, increased the boom in his voice, and asked her, "What did you say?"

"I just want to know what's wrong with her." A tear rolled down Bella's cheek as she looked at me, expecting an answer.

An answer I couldn't give.

Because normal didn't exist in my world anymore.

Because I was unsure of everything.

"Look at her," Bella continued. "Her expression even looks funny."

I slowly turned my head to the right and stared at the antique French mirror that hung on the dining room wall, trying to see what stared back at me. I noticed that my eyes were glassy.

Red.

Confused.

I rubbed my slightly chapped lips together, exposing the one dimple in my cheek, and let the tears that had begun to form freely fall. I still looked like the same ole Oshyn, but I was tired.

Very tired.

"Bella, get your ass up those damn stairs, and don't make me say it again," Brooklyn warned. Realizing that the next time he yelled, he would most likely follow up with his big hand, she got up, with Mye hanging off her side, and rolled her eyes as she carried the toddler along with her.

As if he aggravated her.

Like she did us on a regular basis.

"Oshyn," Brooklyn said before finally blowing out the candles himself. After that he took a seat by my side. "Talk to me. What is all of this about? Your whole attitude seems like it's coming out of nowhere. Everything was cool yesterday, last week, last month. What happened today?"

He was right.

I had changed. Drastically.

I had been fine this whole time and was quite surprised by how easy the transition to the island from the States had been. The culture shock, and the fact that none of us spoke French, were a bit different, but they didn't affect us too much. We weren't a mingling family. I homeschooled Bella, and we never did too much socializing with the natives. We had each other and clung to that as if our lives depended on it, because they did.

We had all coped the best we knew how since the tragedy. While Bella pretended like nothing had ever happened, Brooklyn found ways to bring it up every chance he got. As if he were a detective trying to find a missing piece of his life. Like the night six months ago, when he lost his memory, which was never fully restored. I always told him to count himself blessed, but he didn't see it that way. He just wished he could remember what happened to him, while I wished I had his gift to forget.

"Oshyn," Brooklyn stated.

"What? Just leave me alone!" I fired back.

"Who are you talking to?" he asked, raising his voice, before realizing that I wasn't one of the kids.

I was glad he stopped himself when he did, because that was going to be another argument I didn't feel like having at the moment.

"Leave me alone. Seriously, just leave me alone!"

"No, I'll never leave you alone. Baby, everything is over, and you have nothing to worry about. Chloe is dead, remember? I'm back for good. I'm never going anywhere. I got you. You're safe." His New York accent melted me. And his strong arms were now extended for me to climb into.

"I just wish that I could've seen them bury her so that I could be sure, you know?"

Brooklyn shook his head. "Baby, that bitch

17

is dead, believe me. I was the last one to see her. There was no way she could've survived that fire."

I didn't believe him, and at that moment it was something that I couldn't explain, but fear had come back over my life.

"Relax," he said calmly as he leaned in and lubricated my lips with his. The sweet and spicy taste of his homemade barbecue sauce let me know that he had been secretly meddling in the food.

"Why are you eating the food, while everyone else is starving?" I asked while playfully shoving him off of me.

"Please, you, Bella, and Mye could afford to skip a few meals." He grabbed a small roll that had developed on my stomach and stuck out from my black Gucci tank top, right before I hit him on his shoulder. I was trying to get him away from me while he pulled me closer. "I love it, though," he continued. "I love all this juiciness."

He then grabbed my butt, which was covered in a Gucci khaki skirt and had noticeably spread from a size six to a size eight.

He was right.

Me, Bella, and Mye had put on several pounds since we moved here six months ago. I couldn't tell if it was the stress or the mere fact that Brooklyn cooked every day, or a combination of both, but we were thick.

He grabbed the hand that held my

princess-cut, eleven-carat wedding ring and said, "See, if you gain any more weight, your finger is going to be suffocated and it'll have to be cut off to get the ring off!"

He was right again. My big-ass wedding band had a serious death grip on my ring finger, and I knew I'd have to either lose some weight or get another ring. I'd be pushing for the latter.

"Come here. I have a birthday gift for you," Brooklyn stated.

"Babe, I told you not to worry about getting me anything. I don't need a gift. You're everything I need."

"Ah, shut up and come on."

He forced me up and led me by the hand to our first-floor master bedroom, a distinct T-shaped suite with an extended view of the sea. He placed me on our king-size bed and then walked back to the door to lock it. This was obviously a grown-up gift that he didn't want anyone else to see.

He wasted no time undressing me, starting with my wife beater and bra and continuing nonstop to my khaki skirt and matching panties. As I lay naked on all one thousand counts of our white sheets, I watched him as he pulled his wife beater over his head and his Armani dark denim jeans off of his sexy dark legs. The tables had turned, and he was now standing before me in his well-endowed birthday suit.

I spread open my legs, grabbed his flaw-lessly wavy, brush-cut head, and pulled it to-ward my pussy.

Because that was where he wanted to be.

Because that was where I wanted him to be.

My pussy began to throb at the slight breeze that passed over it, which came from the air flowing from his mouth.

And then he kissed it.

French-kissed it.

He made out with my pussy as if it had been an eternity since the last time he had seen it, making sure to focus on my clit, because that was how I liked it, and he knew it. I arched my back slightly, trying to maintain my compo-sure while he sucked on it.

"Oh my God," were the words I allowed to slither out of my mouth as I found myself in heaven with the man of my dreams.

My soul mate.

My husband.

"What are you trying to do to me?"

I moaned, slightly losing control of the arch in my back and violently jerking, trying to keep myself from cumming while he had me pinned down. He slurped, sucked, and spit in it until I just couldn't take it anymore.

"You . . . have . . . to . . . stop . . . now. . . . Please . . . let . . . go. . . . Don't . . . want . . . to . . . cum . . . now." But my cries fell on deaf ears.

His hold was too tight on me, and I couldn't free myself from his grip. My skin began to glow as my sweat glands sprang into action, and my nipples hardened like rocks.

"Pleaseee, Brooklyn, stop. Come . . . up . . . here," I begged. "Kiss me."

But he wouldn't listen. Instead, he went the opposite way, stopping the lovemaking of my pussy to extend the same courtesy to my French-manicured toes. He took his tongue and ran it smoothly between each toe, taking his time to give each little piggy his undivided attention.

"Shit!" was what I said romantically as I bit my lower lip and laid my head back to stare at our high ceiling. "Shit, shit, shit!"

Who would've thought that toes could feel so good? I wondered as he continued with his journey. Finally, he stopped on the last toe and moved his thick chocolate body on top of mine.

As his face brushed up against mine, I allowed my lips to softly kiss his cheeks. He was perfect in every way, with skin as soft and smooth as Mye Storie's butt. He moved his lips to mine and kissed me softly.

Gently.

Like he was in love with me and he was happy that I was his wife. He stuck his soft, sweet tongue out, and I took it into my mouth hungrily. My head got to bobbing back and forth as I stroked his tongue just as I had his magic stick on plenty of occasions.

And then he kissed me hard.

Passionately.

For a long time.

For what seemed like eternity. And I loved every minute of it. Brooklyn and I had sex every day, and we were so attracted to each other that each time felt like the first. He wanted me as much as I wanted him.

I got wetter as I felt his big black dick getting harder and expanding on my leg. It began to throb and jump as it got near my bottomless pit. He was ready and so was I.

Brooklyn put it in.

I gasped.

And I let out a breath of air as I welcomed him into his home.

"Happy birthday, baby," he whispered as he rocked back and forth on top of me. I wrapped my arms around his back and my legs around his butt as he dug deeper into my pussy.

"Ah, Daddy . . . oh my God, please," was all I could muster as I dug my head into his shoulder as he relentlessly pounded my pussy out.

With each wild stroke, he kissed my face and then my neck and then my breasts, making sure to take his time nibbling on both nipples, giving them both the same amount of time. I threw my pussy at him with each thrust he gave, and came before I wanted to.

"Jesus, that felt so good!" I said, panting heavily.

"Oh yeah?" he murmured as he kept pumping.

He was ready for round two, and I could tell that he had built up lots of energy for this one. I let my hands wander around his body before running my fingers through the crack of his butt and landing them on his hole.

"What the fuck are you doing?" he asked before pulling himself off of me.

He had an obvious attitude.

"I was just playing around, baby. Come back."

But he wouldn't come back. He seemed to be past angry at what I had just done. Although I had never tried anything like that with him before, I made a mental note to never do that shit again.

"I'm sorry," I pleaded, with my bottom lip poked out. "I'll never do that again, I pinkie promise."

I extended my pinkie out as my binding contract and waited, while he just stared at me, still visibly angry. Like he had been violated and this had happened before.

Like I wasn't his wife.

I got off my back and straddled him. His dick had gone a little limp, but I knew that I could get it back up in no time. I rubbed my pussy on it while I kissed him on his neck.

And then his ears.

And then his lips.

I felt the magic wand working as it rose back up to the occasion, and before he changed his mind, I jumped on it and rode it like I was on a wild bull in the Wild, Wild West.

He had forgiven me.

It didn't take long for my bull to cum, and when he did, he yelled out so loud, I just knew the children were going to hear him. I felt every inch of his thousands of babies swim up my stream, trying to hibernate in eggs that would never accept them. My birth control pills would never allow that. More kids were no longer in my future. We lay holding each other in our own sweat and stayed there until both of our breathing patterns had calmed a bit.

"I love you," I let him know after I kissed his wet and salty forehead.

"I love you, too."

"I want to ask you something."

"What's up?"

"Why did you get so angry when I touched you there?" I asked in a soft tone.

I felt his body tense back up.

Like a nerve had been struck.

"I'm a man. Men shouldn't be touched there. It's just not right, so don't do that shit again," he demanded.

"Get your panties out of a bunch. I was just playing with you."

I wanted to tell him that he had been raped and just couldn't remember, but I left it alone. Instead I rushed to get on top of him again, but the phone rang. Brooklyn reached over and picked it up with speed before I could.

"Hello? Who is this?" he screamed, taking his hostility against me out on the caller.

And then, with the phone still glued to his ear, he paused, looked me in my eyes, only to quickly dart his eyes back at the floor. He avoided any kind of eye contact with me. Avoided any kind of questions I was going to have. He fidgeted with the phone for just a little while longer . . . just listening before hanging it up.

"Tomorrow we're going to get this number changed," he said to me. And then the phone started ringing again. "It's probably just some dumb kids playing on the phone."

"Are you sure? Isn't there some way we can get the calls traced?"

This was one of the rare moments when I missed the simpler things in life, such as caller ID. For whatever reason, we didn't have it, and in all actuality we never thought we were going to need it. Guess we assumed that all our troubles were behind us, but I was slowly beginning to think that we were wrong. At this point, I had gotten hyped like I was in a Lifetime movie, trying to think of any solution that would solve this mystery.

"No, Oshyn. Calm down. Just relax. You're overreacting, baby. Just chill out, and I'll take care of changing our phone number first thing in the morning."

"But I know it was her! It was Chloe calling here! What did she say to you?"

The thought of getting my husband to believe me would have made me feel a little better, but my concerns fell on deaf ears. He looked at me with the same stare that I had gotten from him all day.

Like I was crazy.

"Oshyn, for the millionth time . . . chill out. That wasn't Chloe!"

3

Chloe

"There you go!" my nurse, Fay, said after unraveling the last bandage from off my face.

It had been almost two weeks since my plastic surgery, and I was relieved to finally have all that shit off of me. Fay handed me the red mirror that never seemed to be too far from my side and held it up to the right side of my face.

"You look beautiful," she said.

I, however, stared at my face in disgust as soon as I caught a glimpse of the final results.

"You must've been paid to say that stupid shit. Look at me!" I dared her, hardly able to commit to the same task myself.

The cuts and burns hadn't gone away completely but rather had taken on a more plastic appearance.

My face had the texture of rubber.

Not skin.

Accompanied by some of *Flavor of Love* Deelishis's big-ass keloids, I looked like a damn fool. My ear that was cut off had been replaced with a decoy that looked exactly like a decoy.

The nurse, who had watched quietly as I examined myself in disgust, took a few steps back to my side, put the mirror down, and said, "You don't look that bad."

"Fuck you, bitch!" I snapped.

My nurse was drop-dead gorgeous.

The way I used to look.

Dark chocolate was the color that adorned her skin, and her double-D breasts looked to have been done by the finest plastic surgeon in town. Her long, wavy weave fell down to her tailbone, and she had dimples that reminded you of a CoverGirl model's. She was high maintenance, someone who should've been among the A-list stars as opposed to the D-list diseased. I felt like she was taunting me.

I could feel the veins popping out of my neck as I tried with everything I had not to slap her. She was much prettier than I was right now, and I knew that she was taunting me. She was trying to take advantage of the fact that for a moment she looked better than I did. She was lucky I didn't have a weapon on me, because those would've been the last words she ever spoke.

But I also noticed something else.

My face didn't move how it normally did once she took the bandages off. My eyes didn't close all the way, either, and they seemed to well up with tears, despite the fact that I wasn't crying. Numbness filled my mouth area, and even though the nurse was getting on my last nerve, my face remained emotionless.

"My face," I said to her, touching it lightly, trying to cure it myself. "Something is wrong with my face! I can't feel it. . . . Something went wrong!"

I became frantic; I couldn't afford for anything else to go wrong. I had to leave as soon as possible, and I was afraid that was no longer going to happen.

"Well, Chloe, of all the cranial nerves, the facial nerve is most susceptible to injury. You encountered a lot of trauma. And remember, we warned you that there was a possibility that your face could be damaged even further with this cosmetic surgery."

"I don't even know why I'm wasting my time with you. You're just some retarded-ass nurse. Talking to you is like speaking to a child. I want to speak with a real doctor. Now!"

"Excuse me?" she said.

Her facial features worked just fine, because I watched the wrinkles on her forehead curl up, showing the disdain she had for me.

"You heard what I said. Get me a muthafucka in here who knows what the fuck they're doing!"

"What's going on in here? Chloe, what's wrong?"

Tommy.

My security.

An old man who'd also been a patient of the hospital longer than he had hoped. An old man who was responsible for paying all the costs, including my stay here and the plastic surgery. He was a seventy-two-year-old albino man who was battling some form of cancer yet would never tell me which one it was. I really didn't care either way.

"My face!" I cried, trying to be dramatic and realizing that my face didn't line up with my theatrics. Instead of looking sad, I had a pitiful blank stare that said absolutely nothing. "They messed up everything. My face is ruined forever! I'm going to sue all you bastards," I warned Fay.

Those were the words that got her out of my room without saying another word. Hopefully, my real doctor was on the way in.

"But, sweetheart, you look beautiful," Tommy said sincerely.

His words weren't comforting in the least. He was a dying old man who wanted companionship and would say anything to get it. He moved in closer toward me, and as he did, I smelled his stale scent of oldness as it breezed by my nostrils, making me wish that my smelling sense had disappeared as well.

Old man Tommy was unattractive, tall, and so skinny that he was beginning to resemble a skeleton. If I could've guessed it, I'd say that he weighed only a little over one hundred and ten pounds. The skin on his face had begun to droop down, and his eyes had started to sink in. The chemo had taken its toll on his body, and from the looks of it, he wasn't going to last too much longer.

The red, dingy Kangol hat he always wore seemed to boost his self-esteem, because he had it on every time I saw him. I could tell that it was something he wore when he was younger, and now, since the day of death seemed to be fast approaching, he wanted to keep what youth he had left.

Let Tommy tell it, it was love at first sight. The night I was rushed into the emergency room from the warehouse was the night when he had decided to take his own life. It was also the night when his will to live returned, and he made a vow to take care of me for the rest of his life. I could give a rat's ass about his story. As long as he felt the need to take care of me, we would be okay. While I continued to cry a tearless cry, my doctor knocked on the door, which had been left open by Tommy.

"Hey, Chloe," Dr. Kroon said as he made his way over to me. He took his fingers and softly went over his work. "Yup, things seem like they went really well. I'm extremely happy with the progress."

"What the fuck! Am I in the twilight zone? I can't feel my face, the scars look like they've been glazed over with plastic, and my ear looks like a Cabbage Patch doll! Fix it!"

Tommy rubbed my arm in a desperate attempt to calm me down, but I elbowed his cancer-ridden body away from me. He shrieked in pain as he held his stomach and rushed over to a chair on the opposite side of the room.

"Now, Chloe, there's no need for the abusive language or physical violence. We're all adults here who can communicate like adults," Dr. Kroon lectured.

"Fuck you and whatever the fuck you're talking about! Bastard, you can feel your face, so don't tell me how to communicate. I paid a lot of money for this bullshit-ass plastic surgery," I said, then glanced over at Tommy. We both knew his rich ass had paid for it, but my story sounded good.

"Well, I can understand your concern. But tell me, what are you feeling?" Dr. Kroon asked, with his pen and clipboard handy. He was obviously ready to take notes.

"What am I *feeling*? Didn't I just tell you that I couldn't feel anything?"

"Dear, the doctor is only trying to help," Tommy said uneasily in the background.

I turned around and stared at him, but to

no avail. My face still wouldn't move, and everything was beginning to seem pointless.

"The numbness that you're experiencing may mean that a nerve has been pinched or injured. Swelling from the surgery might be putting pressure on the nerve as well." Dr. Kroon paused and stared into my face. "Go ahead and wrinkle your forehead for me." I tried, but from the look on his face, it wasn't moving. "Your eyes seem to be tearing up also," he observed.

"How in the hell are you going to fix this, Doc?" I asked frantically.

"I want to keep you here for a while. I'm concerned that you may have some facial nerve paralysis, which is not unusual for someone who's had as much facial trauma as you have." He paused after seeing the anguish in my eyes. "It will heal, though," he continued. "Trust me. You just have to stay two to three more weeks."

"Stay? I can't stay here. My family needs me," I cried as I placed my fucked-up face into the palms of my fucked-up hands.

Tommy stood up and walked toward my bed. His movements were slow, and I could've sworn I heard bones cracking in the process. I stopped to wonder how he made his millions. He'd told me stories about being an invest-ment banker and stockbroker. But most of it, I didn't believe. Especially the stories about the beautiful women he'd had. Tommy was hard on the eyes, but his pockets were loaded, so what the hell? Whatever he said, I would go along with.

"Doctor, thank you for your help, but can you please leave us alone for a second? I don't want her any more upset than she already is."

Awww, so sweet, I thought, clowning Tommy from my bed. He wanted to protect me . . . fucking sucka. I guess this was his way of letting me know that he had those capabilities.

"Certainly," Dr. Kroon said as he gathered up everything and left the room.

My plan was working just as I thought it would. I began crying harder and louder as Tommy put his frail hand behind my neck, trying his best to console me.

"I just need to be with my family again. My daughter, she . . . she needs me. She's sick, and she needs to be with her mother. Little girls shouldn't grow up without their mothers," I wailed as the tears kept falling down my face.

"Your daughter? You never told me that you had a child," he said to me, sounding disappointed. "I told you that I have a thirty-two-year-old daughter who hasn't spoken to me in years. But you never told me anything about a daughter. Nothing," he added.

His voice carried a tone that said our bond had been broken by me not revealing my whole life to him, as he had to me. His wife dying of cancer not too long before he was diagnosed with his. His daughter, who couldn't wait for him to die so that she could get her inheritance. Something I secretly wished for. I planned on marrying his ass . . . becoming a rich bitch, getting money . . . the kind Anna Nicole Smith lucked up on.

"I'm sorry, Tommy. This is all way too much for me to bear. I don't have the money to pay for her hospital bills, or the money to get to where she is. I need to get to Rochester. I have to see my baby," I began screaming. "I just . . . Maybe I'll just . . . kill myself!"

That was all I could think of before I grabbed my mirror and banged it against the steel post next to my bed, making it shatter everywhere. I grabbed a big piece of my seven years of bad luck and held it over my wrist to let Tommy know that I meant business.

"No, Chloe, don't!" was all I heard him say before I took the sharp glass and ran it across the veins on my wrist, opening up my skin and letting the dark blood trickle down my arm.

Staining my bed.

"Oh my God, somebody please help us!" Tommy shouted out, but not in enough time to stop the second slice of my skin.

My once untainted flesh now hung wide open as the heavy flow of blood continued to spill out. Realizing that no one had come to my aid, Tommy quickly grabbed some of my old cloth bandages from off the edge of my bed and tried his best to hold them tightly against my wounds. It was at this moment I wished I had AIDS.

So he would get infected and die.

But not before I could convince him to leave me his money.

4

Chloe

"Damn. They really fucked you up!" Tuff said when I walked into his house.

It had been two weeks since I left the hospital without being discharged. Once I left on my own, I wasted no time flying into Rochester and catching a cab from the airport to Arnett Boulevard to go through with my plans. Even though my old man, Tommy, wanted me to listen to the doctor's warnings about me not being ready to leave the hospital yet, he still made sure I had as much money as I needed to ensure that my "daughter" got the best health care that was available.

Tommy started me off with eight thousand dollars, which was all he could get his hands on at the moment, and promised to deliver more soon, just as long as I didn't kill myself.

I agreed.

I did a little clothes shopping with the money before leaving Raleigh and decided to save the rest, just in case Tommy didn't come through with his promise or died.

Men could never be depended upon.

That was just a setup for failure.

"What the hell are you talking about? My face is just a little swollen from the surgery, but I look fine," I said, trying to convince him and myself.

I walked over to the full-length mirror he had leaning against his red living room wall, and noticed how much weight I had lost. Damn, where did my ass go? I asked myself silently, making a mental note to eat as much as I could to get my size back up. I was used to being thick in all the right places, and I was going to eat everything in sight to get back to size eight, which I was used to. I refused to resemble anything like Oshyn's skinny ass.

I'm glad it's still summertime, I thought as I straightened out the Alice and Olivia T-shirt I wore and pulled up my Rock & Republic jeans, which seemed to be sagging. I'd gotten so used to North Carolina's weather that I was glad that winter hadn't come yet. My skin could no longer handle the blistering cold of Rochester's winter. The bandage that was wrapped around my wrist after my necessary suicide attempt was still in place, and I just stood there, shaking my head at what a sad sight I was.

"Nah, you definitely fell off, Ma," he continued, snapping me out of my daze. "But I wasn't even talking about the surgery. I'm talking about how Oshyn and Brooklyn fucked you up."

He began to laugh.

My blood began to boil.

"No wonder you trying to find them. I would've made it my life's mission to get them back, too, if my face looked fucked up like yours!"

Tuff bent over and laughed so hard, he didn't seem able to contain himself. I didn't see anything that funny and couldn't believe that he would even play me like that. But he would pay.

"Like I said, faggot-ass nigga, my face is just a little swollen . . . that's all."

"Yeah, and like I said," he repeated as his laughter died down a bit, "you look crazy!"

As strong of a woman as I was, he kept poking at the one insecurity I had at the moment . . . my appearance. *Damn, my shit isn't that bad,* I thought to myself and snuck one more glance in the mirror. My slanted brown eyes were still beautiful, and my skin, despite the war wounds, was still flawless.

My long jet-black hair was bone straight and settled near the bottom of my bra. Luckily, I had thick hair, keeping him from seeing the mutant ear I was desperately trying to hide. I stole myself away from the mirror after mentally building my self-esteem back up and turned my attention back to him.

"Oh, okay. Well, you just wait until my baby, Brooklyn, finds out that his own cousin turned on him. We'll see who has the last laugh then."

At that very moment, it was me who was having the last laugh. Tuff was Brooklyn's first cousin; their mothers were sisters. The whole family hailed from Brooklyn, New York. Tuff was thirty-five and was readjusting to society after taking a ten-year vacation in Attica. A bid he took for Brooklyn.

He'd been out for only a couple of months and decided to move to Rochester instead of going back home because he knew that this was where all the dudes came to get money. But he had a vendetta he wanted to settle. I guess while he was in jail, he heard about the high life that Brooklyn was living, and became salty since he was barely getting by with his commissary money.

But now that he was back out on the streets and had his money right again, this was his time to get Brooklyn back. He had found out where I was through the streets and had reached out to me, letting me know that we had the same goal in mind. The only difference was I was ready to kill. He wasn't.

Tuff was a shorter version of his cousin, standing only five-eleven, definitely too short for my taste, but sorta stylish. They looked alike, though. Both of them had those deep dimples and dark skin. I was sure that when they were younger, they were mistaken for brothers.

Wouldn't have surprised me if that was really the case.

Mothers weren't shit.

That was the one thing we had in common.

He wore black dreadlocks that barely grazed his shoulders and were neatly done. Kept himself up well, though, just like my boo.

"What in the hell are you still laughing at?" he asked me, visibly upset that I had threatened to reveal to Brooklyn that he was my source.

"Who the fuck gave you the name Tuff, anyway? They should've called you Bitch-Ass Nigga instead. You're the worst."

I shook my head, disgusted that I had more balls than he did. Prison had made him soft and afraid to go back, which tainted his ability to move like a real thug moved.

"I told Brooklyn that I was the only friend he had. I tried to warn him that I was the only person on this earth who wouldn't hurt him, but did he listen to me? Noooo! And now what is he left with? He's left with his own sorry-ass cousin turning him in for his own financial gain. That's not how you treat your family," I scolded.

"That nigga left me!" he yelled. "Ten years I did in Attica for him. Ten years for some drugs that weren't even mine!"

He felt the need to explain himself to me, which led me to believe that he felt a little guilty for his betrayal.

"I ought to shoot you in your face myself," was my threat to him. I was sure that Brooklyn still thought he had friends, but this was proof that money was still the only thing that made people cum. After all, a couple of hundreds was all it took for him to rattle off the phone number to me weeks ago.

"Word on the street was right," he said as he picked up a manila envelope off the couch and handed it to me. "Your ass is crazy."

I tore the top of the envelope open before telling him, "Shut the fuck up," and pulled the contents out. I held in my hands three blank pieces of paper. "My patience is really starting to run thin with you, Tuff. What is this shit? Why are all these pages blank?" I asked as I threw them in his face.

I was extremely calm. And if he knew anything about me, he'd be worried at my nonchalance.

"I was thinking. . . ." He put his hand on his chin and rubbed it a little. "If you would do anything to get them back for what they did to you, I'm sure that you wouldn't mind throwing in a couple extra thousand dollars. I have

Brooklyn's whereabouts and other important information right here," he said, tapping on his back pocket.

He grinned, showing the same gap that lived in between Brooklyn's teeth. Showing the same love of money that I had. "Word on the street is that you have plenty of money, and I want what you got," he said.

He turned his back to me as if I didn't matter. As if there was no way to negotiate his new terms. Yeah, I knew I had close to seven thousand to move around with, but the reality of it all was that I was broke. I didn't have a dime to my name, and if it weren't for Tommy, and him falling in love with me at the hospital, I'd be in deep shit.

There was one thing I did have, though, that a man could never turn down—my sex appeal. With him being locked up for ten years, I knew that there was no way he could resist. I crept up behind him and slid my hands up his royal blue Christian Audigier T-shirt. A blind person could tell that he had spent a decade in jail just by the way his body was cut up and toned from all the heavy weight lifting that people with nothing but time on their hands did.

I moved his hair out of the way, closed my eyes, and kissed the back of his neck, while he just stood there, refusing to make a sound. At this point, I wondered if mine was the first woman's touch he'd felt since his release. The more I kissed him, the more he began to resemble his cousin.

I couldn't wait to be in his cousin's arms once again, so I closed my eyes and imagined that Tuff was Brooklyn. My nipples got hard and began poking through the white T-shirt, which I decided to take off, leaving me in my white lace Victoria's Secret bra.

This was what I had amounted to.

Cheap-ass Victoria's Secret.

I made my way in front of Tuff and took off the True Religion jean capris I had on. "Do you like what you see?" I whispered seductively as I placed my arms around his broad chocolate neck.

The sweet smell of Sean John cologne hit my nose as I rubbed my pussy on him. Even though it looked like I had lost a few pounds, when my clothes came off, you could tell that I still had curves, that I'd never lost my shape.

I closed my eyes and parted my lips slightly to finally feel what Brooklyn's lips now tasted like. I was only seconds away from making love to my man, but Tuff's dreads were getting in the way of my daydream. I held them back before I came to the realization that he wasn't the real thing, and I was abruptly pushed out of the way, which quickly snapped me into a harsh reality.

"Please, don't nobody give a damn about

your worn-out pussy," Tuff ranted. "Anybody can get that shit!"

He stopped talking just for a moment to bend down and pick up my clothes off the floor, then forcefully shoved them into my arms.

"Worn-out pussy?" I questioned, catching my clothes tightly in my arms. "Ten years you been letting them niggas bang your pussy out," I said, actually wondering how large his asshole had become.

He didn't allow what he really felt about my comments to show. He stood tall, appearing to be unfazed, as he picked his teeth with a straw he'd pulled from his pocket.

"All I want is my fucking money. You know how this shit goes, baby. You aren't on top anymore. Bow down and pay your respect. It's a new king in town." He smiled again, thinking this shit was funny.

I looked Tuff up and down, with a frown on my face, letting him know that I was disgusted by the smallness of his new "king" status. Was the nigga asking for a blow job?

And then I laughed.

Hard.

"Me? Not on top? Yeah, you've been gone for way too long," I said, trying to explain it to him, still snickering at this last comment. I was still very calm, which surely surprised him as much as it did me. Everyone was so used to me flipping off of emotions, and anything different was out of character for me. "But I can show you better than I can tell you who the boss still is."

"Is that supposed to be a damn threat?" Tuff asked while squaring up on me. I guess his huge, flex-the-muscle scare tactic was something that had worked while he was locked up, but it only caused more chuckles out of me.

"Nah, not a threat, baby. I don't make threats."

"You know what it is," he told me, muscles still flexed.

"Whateva, nigga."

He didn't scare me.

Rochester was my city.

The place where I was born and bred. And I'd be damned if I was going to let a bitch-ass Brooklyn nigga come in and mark his spot in my territory. I had more balls than he did, and today was the day that he'd die with them in his mouth.

My high of getting some dick was immediately replaced with the insatiable desire to get rid of him. Those were the only images I saw while I slipped my T-shirt and capris back on. He turned his back on me and walked over to his pack of Newport cigarettes, which lay open on the coffee table.

He had put his guard down and had underestimated me.

Bad mistake.

Huge.

I quietly picked up the small steel baseball bat that lay behind his couch. I'd caught a glimpse of it when I first walked in the house. While his fingers flickered with the lighter as he attempted to light his cigarette, I crept up behind him and cracked him over the head as hard as I could with the baseball bat.

In slow motion, the cigarette dropped to the floor.

He wasn't too far behind.

Tuff dropped to his knees, and when I made my way to his back pocket, I saw the blood trickling down his face. I dug inside his pocket, grabbing the piece of paper, which was neatly folded up, and quickly unraveled it. *Jackpot,* I thought as I read Brooklyn's address. The pain seemed to shock Tuff to a point where he wasn't moving and hadn't said a word. I guess it didn't take too long for him to see things my way.

Robbing him of any final words that a man scheduled to die was supposed to get, I banged the steel bat harshly against the front of his face. I listened to his skull crack open and felt the warm blood splatter against my skin every time I swung. All thirty-six times.

The shit felt good.

So I kept swinging.

Until I was sure he had crossed over to the other side.

However, at that point I still wasn't satisfied.

Rage took over, so I stomped toward the kitchen.

This muthafucka better have a decent knife.

I wanted to make sure his ass was dead, so I vowed to stab him until he was cut into tiny pieces.

5

Oshyn

"Where is he? You took my baby! Tell me where he is, or I swear to God I'll kill you!" I screamed.

I straddled him in the bed, trying my best to cut off his blood circulation with my legs as I held the butcher knife up to his neck. The tears streamed down my face as I desperately tried to find where Mye Storie had gone.

I saw the fear in Brooklyn's eyes as he lay on his back with his hands in the air. Since I'd climbed on top of him in his sleep, he had remained speechless, but then he found the nerve to somehow whisper, "Baby, please, don't do this. The kids are fine and—"

I put more pressure on his neck.

The knife was beginning to cut through.

"Stop it! Stop with all your fucking lies! You killed him! You killed the only son I had left!"

I had become hysterical, deranged almost, but for good reason. I was a mother who fought for her children, because that was the only way they stayed safe. But I seemed to have failed again. Mye was gone, and I was sleeping with the enemy. "I'll kill you if—"

Before I was able to finish my sentence, Brooklyn snatched my head into his arms and yanked me into a headlock while I was still on top of him. My long cream satin nightgown got in the way as I tried desperately to get back the knife, which had fallen off the side of the bed.

He held me and hugged me hard while I squirmed to break free. The beads of sweat that started popping out of his pores were now smeared on my face as he held me tighter, forcing me to inhale the Dove soap he'd used not too long ago to wash my sex off of his body. I found myself getting weaker and squirming a little less as the tears mixed with snot trickled into my mouth.

"It's going to be okay," my husband promised me as he gently laid my head on his shoulder and stroked my long hair back into its original place. "Everything is all going to be okay."

Lies.

Those were all lies.

I decided to take advantage of the situation while he still had my head buried in his armpits. My mouth opened wide, and I took a big chunk of his meat into it and bit down as hard as I could.

"Ahhh!" was all you heard. The sound echoed off the four walls of our room. Brooklyn forcefully pushed me off of him and onto the floor. "What the fuck is wrong with you, Oshyn? It's six o'clock in the morning, and you're acting like a—"

His missing word was replaced with quick movement when he realized what I had back in my possession. He found himself on the other side of the bed just seconds before I swung at him. My thrust was fast, but it wasn't quick enough, because the end result was a puncture wound in our Vera Wang king-size mattress instead of in his skin.

"Oshyn! Give me the fucking knife!"

Although he was on the other side of the bed, his hands were extended toward me, and his tone was that of a negotiator. He had obviously never perfected his negotiating skills, or he would have known that kind of tone would set me off. For his sake, he needed me to be as calm as possible. This was now a hostage situation, which Brooklyn thought he was going to be able to talk me out of.

But he was wrong.

Dead wrong.

"You . . . took . . . my . . . baby!"

The steady flow of warm tears that streamed down my face mimicked the falls at Niagara Falls. All I wanted was answers, and he wasn't giving them to me. I started walking around the bed, trying to get closer to him, and he in turn started walking in the other direction.

"Stop and think about what you're doing right now." He squirmed a little as he touched the huge bite mark I'd left on him. "Bella and Mye are still asleep. I didn't kill anybody. Just put the knife down. I'll take you to where they are."

I felt myself hyperventilating, so I put my head down for a moment to catch my breath. Before I could look back up, Brooklyn had leaped across the bed and had thrown me to the floor, taking the knife right out of my hand.

Unable to pick myself up from the cold chocolate hardwood floors, I just lay there, wondering when all this pain was going to end. I looked up and noticed that Brooklyn was gone. I wasn't sure where he went, but when he came back, there was nothing in his hand that I could hurt anyone with. He scooped me up off the floor and into his strong arms and laid me back on the bed.

Like I was originally.

Before all of this began.

When he laid his body on top of mine, I was surprised at how weightless his body felt. "Get off of me!" I demanded.

I really didn't mean those words, which was proven by my not putting up a fight. I was slowly snapping out of whatever state of mind I had put myself in. He said nothing back. Just covered me like a blanket, trying to force me to go back to sleep.

Like I was a baby who needed to be pacified.

"Oshyn," he said.

I ignored him, but he wouldn't give up.

"You've been through things that no human being should ever have to experience, and you've done it with no one to really talk to and help you through these times." He paused, waited for me to respond, and when I didn't, he continued. "Baby, you know that you always have me to talk to, but I don't think that I can bring you through the demons you're dealing with. You're going to have to go to counseling."

I shifted my body from side to side while he was still on top of me, uneasy about the words that were coming out of his mouth. "I'm fine now," I assured him. "I'm sure I was just having a bad dream, but everything is all right now. I don't need counseling."

He shook his head, but not before blurting out, "No, you're not okay. I'm pretty sure that mental health is on my insurance. But even if it isn't, I'll pay the expenses no matter how much it costs, for however long you need it. I'll do whatever it takes to get back the Oshyn I fell in love with."

"So you're not in love with me?" I asked, confused about his last remark. "Am I not the same Oshyn?"

"Of course I'm still in love with you, but something is wrong, and we have to figure it out. The kids need you. I need you. So, like I said, money is no object . . . whatever it takes."

Brooklyn made great money at the hotel, enough money to pay all the bills himself, allowing me to be a full-time mother. Rooms at that expensive five-star hotel had to be booked months in advance, and it was a place where all the clients had black cards. They even had ports where helicopters brought their guests to private parties in villas. In this town the main way of getting money was through tourism. And in this town everyone who worked in the hotel industry was able to afford a more than decent lifestyle for their family.

I snapped out of my thoughts and found myself bursting into tears. Depression seemed to be hitting me hard, and it wasn't a burden I felt I could tackle by myself.

"Shhh, it's going to be okay," Brooklyn promised.

"I just miss Chloe so much," I revealed.

"You tried, though. You tried your best to get rid of her, and she didn't deserve any of it!"

Even in my deranged state, I watched once again as sadness filled my husband's eyes, along with his curiosity about my health and sanity. I placed my hands on his chest and pushed him off of me, quickly getting myself off the bed before he could put me back on it.

"What are you doing?" he asked as he watched me go into my closet and throw all my clothes on the floor.

"I'm packing my bags. Going back to the States. Need to find Chloe and talk to her." I was frantically running around, trying to put something together and into a suitcase.

"But she's dead, babe. She's gone forever."

"No. She never died. You didn't kill her."

He put his head down like a puppy who had just chewed up a new pair of Christian Louboutin stilettos and knew that he was in for an ass whupping. I knew that this was the best time to get some kind of truth out of him.

"Tell me the truth, Brooklyn! I already know it. I just want you to say it out loud, that it was Chloe that was calling here the other day!"

Silence.

He never lifted his head back up.

"Please stop making me out to be crazy. For the sake of my sanity, tell me the truth!" I said, trying to drill the guilt into his head. "Tell me who was on the other end of the phone that night."

He slowly brought his head back up, barely making eye contact, and parted his lips enough to say, "You're right. It *was* Chloe on the phone. She's still alive."

6

Chloe

Finally.

Living good again.

I lay stretched out on my lounge chair, feeling the effects of my third mojito, as I watched my sweet and savory man, Brooklyn, make drinks behind the bar. He looked good. Damn good. I guess the time spent away from him had made me forget how sexy he really looked in his clothes. His bulging arms, tight waist, and firm abs made me squirm all across the cushion. Maybe it was all the white he wore, which made his muscles appear larger and sexier than before.

Then again maybe it wasn't the color of his clothes. My skinny waiter had on white, too, yet was so thin that he looked like he'd just finished smoking a pound of crack. He'd been by my private section a few times, asking if I wanted another drink. Kept bragging about the bartender, talking about how good he was, and how even the locals crowded his bar every day for his famous creations. I wanted to tell Rosario, or whatever the fuck his crazy-ass name was, that I was well aware of how good the bartender was. I wanted to tell him that I knew Brooklyn very well and would be fucking him in front of his dead wife by the end of the night.

Instead, I tilted my tan, oversize floppy hat and lifted my cup of ice as soon as I saw him headed my way. That should've given him the clue that I was good for the moment. I needed peace . . . just time to monitor Brooklyn's every move. The spot I'd chosen proved to be perfect. I sat about seven yards away, underneath a large umbrella and with a five-foot-three partition in front of me. It was a fake-me-out private cabana, but it worked well. I knew it would be difficult for him to see me laid back on the plush lounge chair, draped in my incognito gear. Especially since his bar was packed . . . and he, crazy busy, was making one drink after another for the loud bar hoppers. Luckily, the pool was behind me and kept the extra noise away.

It was nearly ninety-eight degrees, so my body adhered to the weather. My sexy two-piece held together by two skinny strings would've driven any man to his knees, especially if I decided to take off the matching sarong that straddled my thighs. I remained still, showing off the tanned skin of my bare, oily legs. It was all I would show for the moment. I didn't want to attract any unnecessary attention. My purpose was to watch Brooklyn like a hawk through my retro, oversize sunglasses until he got ready to leave work and head home.

While I watched him, my glamour thing obviously attracted a little bit of attention. The expensive Dolce & Gabbana shades, my freshly polished toes, the four-hundred-dollar Bottega Veneta pumps, and my freshly waxed pussy made me a target. Although I stayed far away from the action around the bar, it seemed as if I attracted some unwanted attention from one of the vendors opposite the bar.

Maybe it was the way my boobs sat nipple first, greeting everyone. It was puzzling, almost scary. I wasn't sure why this deeply dark-skinned woman with a crib-sized sheet wrapped around her head was eyeing me from afar. When my eyes got a chance to examine her small white tent and the contents, I became curious. The sign read SEE YOUR FUTURE. I thought, *Bullshit.* I'd rather spend my money with the jewelry guy, or the lady with the hand-painted mask. At least I could scare the shit out of Oshyn.

It seemed every chance the woman got, she would wave me over with her hand. I just closed my eyes, because her sales pitch was whack. The glare spelled evil. . . . She didn't crack a smile and never even made a move. She just sat staring, waiting for me to open my eyes again. I thought about moving but was distracted by Brooklyn taking off his linen shirt. He had apparently spilled something red on his shirt and was now in a tight white wife beater.

Damn, I shouted inside, then raised my hand to block the strong rays from the sun.

The ugly bitch still stared but needed to be blocked from my mind. *It is all about Brooklyn,* I told myself, slipping my hands into my bikini bottom. I closed my eyes, ready to dream. To feign. Ready to get my thing off. I thought about me and Brooklyn on the beach.

Alone.

Words couldn't express how horny I got when I got the vision of his body on top of mine. It was me and him grinding right on the lounge chair, right on the beach. "Oh hell yeah," I whispered to myself.

The more my body moved, the hornier I became. Even with my eyes closed tightly, the scene seemed so surreal. My fingers massaged my smooth, bald pussy briskly, while my mouth fought hard not to shout out. Lately, I had become the queen of masturbation, and I now held the world record on cumming from a finger. But Brooklyn always brought out the best in me.

I thought about the ice in my cup and

opened my eyes to grab a few cubes. Something new, something different always sparked my interest. I was still in the zone but wanted to take it a step further. My vagina throbbed for a dick, a hard one . . . but fingers and ice would have to do. I was already wet but needed to get soaked. I moved a little more, squirming in the seat, and allowing each cube to press against my clit.

The coldness excited me. Had me going wild. I didn't give a fuck who saw me or my weird facial expressions. I kept grinding and swaying my hips from side to side, while melting pieces of ice with my hot pussy. The shit felt so damn good, I was willing to cum with or without Brooklyn. Just when I was about to cum, I got creative and inserted a piece of ice into my pussy, pretending it was the best dick I'd ever had. Of course, it melted. Then I took a deep breath as I nutted inside my bathing suit and all over the seat. The shit was so good. I reached for another piece of ice but was interrupted by the ringing of my cell phone. It said UNKNOWN. I hated that shit and hated that somebody was trying to sabotage my sex life.

"What!" I shouted into the phone.

"Chloe, what's wrong? I was calling to check on you." Tommy's voice sounded concerned, and even though I knew he meant well, I just wasn't the compassionate type.

"How can I help you?" I snapped.

"You okay? I haven't heard from you since you left the hospital."

"I didn't want to get you involved. This is too much for you to handle," I told him with sorrow. "My baby . . . my baby . . . my baby," I kept repeating. "I'm not sure how things are gonna turn out."

"Chloe, listen to me . . . ," Tommy began.

"No, you listen to me!" I flipped out, sat straight up, and decided playing games wasn't on the agenda for the day. "I need ten thousand and fast!" I shouted. "I'll explain later, but if you plan on being with me, send it through Western Union. Today!" I barked.

"But . . . but . . . but . . . Chloe—"

"No buts . . . you old fucker! If you wanna run with a bad bitch, get that money sent. If not, stay on the porch and I'll see you when I see you."

There was silence.

Then breathing.

Maybe he'd had a heart attack and left me his money, anyway. Then that thought was quickly ruined. "Ten thousand," he confirmed in a meek tone.

"Exactly." My tone showed no remorse. And he knew I meant business. "I'll be back at home in a few days," I added, using my sweet voice. "I got something for you, Daddy," I sang, then hung up and turned to my left.

There she was again. Sitting. Staring. Every time we made eye contact, it became more obvious she was watching me just as much as I was watching her.

"Come. Let me share your future!" she shouted in her light foreign accent.

I hopped up angrily, pulled my sarong tighter, and waltzed over toward the tent. As I got closer, a bizarre feeling came over me. Almost warning me not to buck at the woman and not to sit down. I looked back over my shoulder at Brooklyn, only to see him shaking a container back and forth, and grinning from ear to ear at the slut leaning toward his frame.

"You like?" The old woman spoke in a ghostly tone. "Sit down," she told me.

Instantly, an eerie feeling came over me. I quickly scanned the two tables underneath the tent, noticing small clear jars labeled HEALING POTIONS, UNLIT CANDLES, and STRONG, ODOROUS POWDERS scattered about. Even tiny red particles, which reminded me of crushed red peppers, covered the small table topped with an old white lace tablecloth.

"Sit, sassy girl, and look into my eyes."

She was an old woman—my guess, in her late seventies—with tons of lines running across her face. I had never let another bitch scare me . . . ever . . . but she was working on making me a punk. First, my eyes darted toward one of her signs. WISE ONE, it read. I looked at her.

She looked back at me.

Hesitantly, I sat in the only wobbly white chair available. It was lopsided and felt like she'd owned it for years. As soon as I sat down, the bitch pulled out a jar of more of that red shit and swiftly started sprinkling it on me.

I flipped. "What the fuck, old lady!"

"It's love powder, my dear." She blew it on me. "Believe me, it will bring you love, money, and power," she said slowly.

Of course, I calmed down. "Any man I want?" I asked, with a smirk that spread about my face.

"Any man," she confirmed.

"How much is this shit?" I asked while going into my bra.

She paused, which gave me a chance to get a good look at her frail skin. Her arms lacked moisture . . . my assumption was from working in the sun daily. And her eyes were sunken in, allowing her bubbly eyeballs to bulge even more. A piece of her wool-like hair peeked out from under her wild-looking scarf. And the long African dress, which fell well below her ankles, didn't add much to her style, either.

"Ten for the basics," she finally said. "Twenty for the good stuff, and thirty if you want to know how to control your men."

"This shit is a scam. I knew I shouldn't have come over here!"

"You think?" she challenged me with her voice. "I have the power to bring good or bad."

"Ohh . . ."

All of a sudden she grabbed my hand tightly, as if the intent was to rough me up for my money. I simply closed my fist and gave her the look of death.

"I'll give you twenty," I told her.

"Your life," she said, gazing into my eyes and squeezing my hand tighter. "Your palm tells me there are two men."

My eyes lit up. Then, once again, I checked on Brooklyn. "Take the thirty," I told her, slapping a twenty and a ten on the table.

She released her grip, took the money, and sat it off to the side with the other money in her small metal box. My first thought, *This lady's making a killing*. The stack seemed to contain roughly three to four hundred bills. I tried to count further but was interrupted by the tightness of the grip she'd got on both my hands.

"Two men. Both good-looking. Both in love with you," she ranted. "One man you know. The other you will soon meet."

Her words made my heart thump.

"Amazing sex. And money," she mumbled to herself.

Now she was talking some shit that I wanted to hear.

"Amazing sex?" I questioned with a smile.

"Yes. Who's this guy I see with you? He's tall, a dark man." She said a few other words, but with a much stronger accent, so I couldn't comprehend. But I'd heard enough. I was sold.

"Oh shit, you are real!" I shouted. *The bitch is describing Brooklyn,* I told myself, shocked. "Tell me more. Are we married! A baby! What? Tell me!"

"Oh . . . noooo . . . noooo," she uttered, with a disappointing shake of her head. "He's with another lady now. But there is someone else for you. He has money, too."

"That's what I want to hear. Positive shit. Nothing negative," I instructed.

"Money is good. But things won't go so good for you. You need some of my powder," she added while sprinkling some more of that bullshit on me before I could dodge it.

"That's enough," I warned.

"No, really. Somebody will pay you back," she continued in a chilling tone. "You've done something really bad, but your payback will be greater. Death, I see death," she repeated.

I tried to pry her hand off of mine. "I said that's it! Now, shut the fuck up, old lady!"

"My mouth may close, but it doesn't change your fate. Ill-fated love affair," she chanted. "Ill-fated love affair."

Without hesitation, I kicked at her feet with force. At the same time, my eyes darted from right to left to see who was watching us nearby or from afar. It was at that moment that I saw him leaving. It was my man in a hurry, leaving work like something was wrong. Like he'd seen a ghost or some shit.

Immediately, I kicked the woman even harder. It didn't take long for her to loosen her grip and for me to snatch her small box holding the money. As soon as I had the loot, *her money,* successfully in hand, we locked eyes. I was already on my feet and moving, but I still couldn't dodge the horrible-smelling dust she blew my way.

"A hex is what you've caused me to do," she said angrily. "My revenge will come at the hands of someone else, but you will die and burn in hell forever," she warned.

"Oh yeah, well, I'll meet you there," I countered as I fled the scene.

I wanted to shout back some more, letting her know I didn't believe in hexes, roots, or any of that shit, but decided against it. With the old woman's money in hand, I jetted toward the parking lot, hoping I hadn't left anything behind. My money was in my bra, and my purse was in the car I'd rented, so whatever Rosario could steal and sell was all his. I had to catch Brooklyn, who was racing from the lot in the Range Rover he drove.

By the time I'd hopped in the rental car, Brooklyn was out of sight. I was still huffing and puffing, trying to catch my breath, as I turned the steering wheel frantically. Passing car after car, I dodged, swerved in and out of traffic, searching for a glimpse of his truck.

The full chase was on his black ass, yet it wasn't enough. Then my breakthrough came. I saw the back of his truck about ten cars ahead of me, turning by a large bend. I sped up, then forced a few cars into the dirt on the side of the road. *He's not gonna outsmart me,* I told myself, wiping off particles of the bullshit the voodoo bitch had sprinkled on me.

Then I heard it.

A fender bender ahead.

Some bitch had hit three old ladies in a station wagon, causing a six-car pileup and causing my man to disappear . . . again.

7

Oshyn

I waited outside, pacing on our narrow driveway, while I looked for any sign of Brooklyn pulling up. Mye got increasingly heavier as I pulled him up on my hip. It was late in the evening, and the temperature was still a scorching ninety-eight degrees, with no signs of letting up.

"Mye, let go!" I demanded as he eagerly managed to grab a chunk of my hair, tangling a few strands in his chubby little hands. Drool began to drip down to the rolls of his shirtless stomach while he laughed at my frustration.

"Bella, come and get your brother!" I yelled.

No answer.

I gave her the benefit of the doubt, because I was all the way outside and she might not have heard me. But I sort of knew that wasn't the case.

"Bella!"

"What?" she sassed, making her presence known at the front door. She stepped outside in her pink Juicy Couture sundress, which gave her the look of an angel, even though she was anything but.

"What?" I repeated softly, though I was angry deep inside.

I thought that her talking-back situation had been cleared up six months ago, and I couldn't quite figure out why it was resurfacing as a problem now. I hated to think it, but maybe Brooklyn had a good point about us going to counseling. Judging from Bella's attitude, and where I assumed it was headed, it wouldn't hurt. It had begun to rain, and although Mye was enjoying the raindrops, I wanted to keep him dry.

"Here. I need you to take Mye with you inside the house. Play with him some. . . . Just keep him out of this rain and out of my hair for a while."

I extended my baby to her, making the choice to ignore the argument that we would have if I mentioned how she'd spoken to me. At this point in my life, I had bigger issues to deal with, and I wanted to choose my battles wisely.

It had been about half an hour since Brooklyn had called in a panic. He'd said he was leaving work and rushing home . . . and had some news to tell me. I knew I couldn't take much more. The voices were back, and this time I didn't want to hear them alone. My grandma, my mother, Apples, and Micah had all returned to me once again, trying to warn me about something that left me tossing and turning during my nap.

Their presence, which once had filled me with comfort and warmth, today left me frightened and alone. I had to admit, I hadn't been myself lately, but I knew this time I needed help before I snapped.

"Whatever," was what Bella blurted out after taking my son. She rolled her little green eyes and turned to go back inside the house. "I'm tired of watching him. You're the mom. . . . That's your job!"

I tried hard to ignore her, but this time it wasn't happening. I snapped.

"Come back here!" I shouted like Joan Crawford in the movie *Mommy Dearest*. My face was balled up into a serious knot, and my fists were balled tightly down by my sides. "You hear me!" I warned.

As soon as Bella was within a few feet of me, I grabbed Mye out of her arms, dropped him on the wet grass, which cushioned his fall, and reached for the back of her rain-soaked sundress. After noticing her trying to get away, I yanked her scrawny ass backward and punched her in her side with all the strength my fist could muster up. I hit her like she was a grown woman, because that was what she acted like. Miss Bella needed to be taught a lesson.

"Owwww!" was the constant noise that escaped out of her mouth, and it now matched Mye's screams.

He had managed, in all his confusion, to crawl to me, only to have me shoo him away like a fly. His cries only got louder as I locked my fingers in her light brown, spiraled hair and pulled, with every intention of making her bald.

"Pleaseeee . . . I'm sorry," Bella confessed as her fair skin turned the color of a Red Delicious apple. Her little hands did what they could to pry mine off of her, but with every attempt she made, I yanked harder. "Please . . . let . . . go!"

That was the last thing I heard before I wrapped my other hand around her throat. Before her little lungs began gasping for air. Before she struggled to inhale the air that freely floated past her. Before she could no longer breathe. At the same time that I was on a mission to kill, a crack of thunder sounded in the air, and a heavy downpour of rain gushed from the sky without warning.

While I choked Bella like a stranger on the streets, my ears flipped outward when the sound of screeching tires was heard. Seconds later Brooklyn pulled up in the Range Rover like a madman. Without hesitation, he jumped from the car and tried to pry me off of Bella. His strength was unbeatable, but I sure as hell tried. Before I knew it, Brooklyn had overpowered me and had set Bella free. Soaking wet, I panted, sweated, and resembled a crazy woman detained in the wet grass, sitting with my hands behind my back.

Mye stopped his wailing only after being rescued by his daddy and looked on as Bella coughed violently. While she attempted to get her regular breathing pattern back, I sat defiantly in the soaking wet grass. We all behaved like a bad storm wasn't really brewing. Well, then again, none of us were normal at the moment. I couldn't believe that I had snapped like that, but hopefully, she had learned her lesson. Otherwise, it was clear that I would do it again, with no one to stop me.

While Brooklyn rushed the kids inside to get dry, I remained outside, pacing in our tiny front yard, trying to make sense of what was happening with me.

My mind was an empty canvas.

With remnants of going senile.

I stood in place, emotionless, watching the rain alternate between mild to gushes of water. If I didn't know any better, I'd say that things couldn't get any worse than this, but I knew better and that thought was just too good to be true.

About ten minutes went by before Brooklyn

emerged from the house. He stood in front of me, scratching his head and uttering the words "I don't know." He looked down at the ground and continued scratching an itch I knew didn't exist. I watched him, trying my best to decipher what his statement meant.

All my frustrations got so heavy that my tears started pouring out without giving me a chance to prepare for them. His scratching finally came to an end, and he stepped forward, grabbing me into his arms, where I felt safe.

"I don't know," he whispered once again, pulling me tighter into his embrace. "I got news that my cousin, Tuff, died," he informed me slowly. "Killed . . . stabbed over forty times. Found dead in his home. He was there for, like, two days," he said, getting choked up. "And then I come home to this."

His shocking news stopped me in my tracks, and I suddenly felt bad about not being able to control my situation. I realized how much stress I'd been putting on him.

"I'm so sorry, baby."

I unconsciously wiped my nose on his wet linen work shirt, leaving it with the remains of my sadness. The rain seemed to slow up a bit, which made me ask if he wanted to go inside.

He ignored my comment.

"He was only thirty-five, the only cousin I had," Brooklyn said with a strained voice.

We stood in the front yard, hugging like

two lovers in the rainstorm who needed one another, until Brooklyn got silent, as if he was daydreaming about his cousin. His eyes were glossy, and he looked into the cloudy sky, just staring, thinking, hurting. I wanted to help him but didn't know what to say.

Tuff was his first cousin, and although he was just a few years older than Brooklyn, he had treated him like he was his father, before getting locked up and having to do a ten-year bid. I wasn't sure if they had talked much since his release a few months ago, but I knew that he was someone Brooklyn held dear to his heart.

"She has a phone call," Bella said, peeking her head out the door. She deliberately ignored me and addressed Brooklyn only.

"Take a message," Brooklyn told her, unable to handle any more drama for the day. "I have to go to Rochester to help with the funeral arrangements," he then said to me.

I kept thinking about Tuff. "You never told me that Tuff lived in Rochester." I had a puzzled look on my face. "I don't understand what would make him go to Rochester after spending all that time upstate."

"Yeah. He didn't want to go back to Brooklyn. He said there was too much trouble there. But, anyways, I'm going to need for you and the kids to come with me. After walking into the mess I just saw, I can't leave you here alone with them."

My jaw hung low.

He talked to me like his trust in me had completely dissolved. Why would he offend me like that? Like I was a mother who would harm her children?

"Let's hurry," he ordered, confirming that I was leaving Saint-Tropez with him.

I guess I didn't have much of a choice.

8

Chloe

The rain came down.

Torrentially.

The kind of downpour that made you look like you had been swimming all day, even if you were in it for a few seconds. The volume of water that fell from the sky seemed to come from nowhere, as it was only just fifteen minutes prior that I was chilling in sunny conditions. And as I vividly remembered the forecast, it was supposed to remain sunny and clear all day.

Fucking liars, I accused the weathermen as I struggled to keep up with Brooklyn. I had already lost him once but had managed to catch back up with him after driving on two wheels and on the wrong side of the road. I desperately hoped that he was leading me to where he lived. *They* lived. The bitch Oshyn lived.

Tuff had gotten over on me when I initially got the address from him. It was the address to Brooklyn's job and not their home. I made a mental note to have somebody spit on the nigga at his funeral. Although I had reservations about how everything would go down, ten minutes later Brooklyn pulled into the driveway of a big, beautiful house.

"Jackpot," I said to myself. They were living large. Just as Oshyn had always done, and as much as I hated to admit it, their house was surprisingly gorgeous.

The sight of Brooklyn fanatically running from his truck snapped me back into reality as I realized what was going on.

Bella's feet were off the ground.

Oshyn's hands around her neck.

I chuckled as I watched the man of the house stop a catfight between a child and a grown-ass woman. *Just like Oshyn,* I thought to myself. *Always trying to scare somebody smaller than her.* I recalled the day in the bookstore when a chick spit in her face and she didn't do anything. *Fuckin' sucka!*

I looked on as Brooklyn grabbed his son off the ground and led Bella, who was gasping for air, into the house. Even though I should've killed the little bitch when I had the chance, she was turning into a beautiful girl. Reminded me of me when I was that age. *Maybe it's not too late to put her on the payroll,* I contemplated, always thinking of a way to come up.

With Brooklyn making sure the kids were safe in the house, Oshyn was left by herself outside. Where it was just me, her, and nothing but time. The rain continued to fall hard, soaking Oshyn and causing her clothes to cling to her body. The wipers barely gave me enough visibility to notice that she had gained some weight. She wasn't fat, but thick.

Just how Brooklyn liked it.

Just how Brooklyn liked it on me.

Her hair was drenched, but I saw that it was longer than mine was, and even though she seemed to be stressed about something, she still looked like money. I fought the urge to hop out of the car and handle her once and for all, because I needed to remember that my time would come. I needed to make sure that it would be perfect.

Not deterred by the storm, Brooklyn came back out of the house and they began to talk. Since my car wasn't a familiar one in the neighborhood, I felt like a parked car with the windshield wipers on was drawing unwanted attention, so I quickly turned them off. And was left with foggy, steamy windows.

I couldn't see them.

They couldn't see me.

Reminded me of the days I used to enjoy having sex in the car. While it rained as hard as it was raining today, I turned on the air conditioner and waited as it defogged the windows. It seemed pointless to sit outside, blindly stalking, but it would be all worth it at the end of the day. I honestly couldn't believe that I was able to get this close to her so soon. I thought that it was going to take some time, even years, before I got a chance to go through with my revenge. But here it was a short six months later and I was in front of her house.

This time she would die.

Oshyn and her whole family.

I contemplated leaving their son, Mye, out of this, but he had both of their blood running through his veins. A line I had to be cut because I couldn't risk him carrying on their name. Harmless now would turn into dangerous later, and I couldn't let that happen. He was just a casualty of war, like his big brother, Micah, had been. My intentions for Bella were to bury her alive. To know that she would be six feet under, suffocating from dirt, warmed my heart.

And Brooklyn, my sweet Brooklyn, would get one more chance. He would be with me or he would be with no one. The choice was his. If he chose to stay with me, we would live happily ever after, like I dreamed. We would go back to the way things were when he would come home and make love to me.

When *we* were in love.

Before Oshyn found out and ruined it all.

But if he chose to stay with her, death would

do them part in a million little pieces, literally. I would chop their bodies up and spread the pieces all over whatever city I decided to kill them in.

I continued to daydream and contemplate how I was going to flawlessly execute my plan and get away with their demise. The last of my family. After them, there was no more heritage until I reproduced.

The heavy rain continued to hit the car, and my thoughts shifted to the old lady who read my palms. I still had no idea where her spooky ass had come from, and even though I didn't believe in that shit, a part of me wished that the thought of me actually being in love wasn't too good to be true.

I closed my eyes and envisioned my mystery man being tall, dark, and handsome, like Brooklyn, but better. I couldn't wait to get Oshyn out of the way so that I could finally get on with my life and start a family of my own.

A crack of thunder blasted through the sky, frightening me and snapping me from my thoughts. I glanced at the time on my dashboard and realized that a little over an hour had gone by since I first parked my car in front of the house and that everyone had gone inside. There wasn't any movement in the house, so I got antsy. It wasn't just their house that seemed motionless, but the whole neighborhood looked desolate.

Eerie.

As if they knew that something was getting ready to pop off. If they knew what I knew, they were better off inside, because my wrath was bigger and stronger than the rainstorm. I decided to pick up my international Black-Berry and call the house.

It rang.

Twice.

"Hello?" Oshyn said.

Oshyn's voice still sounded the same as I listened to her tell Brooklyn, "She's still calling." It was beyond me why they hadn't changed the phone number yet, but she had never been too swift when it came to commonsense shit. I hung up the phone and sat back for several minutes to relax a little. My patience was beginning to run thin when I noticed something through my car window. The rainstorm had refused to clear up, and I struggled to see past the glass that I looked through.

With strained eyes, I looked on as Brooklyn and Oshyn rushed out of the house to put a few big suitcases in their truck. *What in the hell is going on here?* I wondered as I watched Bella run out of the house and quickly throw her pink suitcase in with the rest of the bags. They all seemed to be incredibly unfazed by the massive rainstorm, which by now had them all completely drenched. Oshyn and Bella jumped in the car, and I watched Brooklyn as he ran back into the house and back out with their son.

The son that he was supposed to have with me.

The son she killed.

The son that I would return the favor to.

While he locked the front door to the house, I couldn't help but wonder if they knew I was in the rental car, stalking them. Did the frequent phone calls to the house give me away? *Why else would they be leaving in such a hurry?* I asked myself, wondering if Tuff had tipped them off. It was like I had always said before . . . No one was to be trusted.

No one seemed to notice my car parked in front of their house as they backed out of their driveway and drove right past me. Refusing to be left behind, I cranked up my car and followed right behind them, being careful not to tail too closely. My windshield wipers squeaked as the rain became more intense again. Although I could barely see anything that was in front of me, the storm turned out to be a great camouflage.

I followed them up and down the rough and narrow alleys that their country called streets, and had a less than smooth drive on the bumpy cobblestone-paved roads.

Beep! Beep! Beeppp!

The horn of the Range Rover sounded as a woman with two young kids crossed the street without a care. Brooklyn dodged the potential catastrophe and slammed on the brakes, while I pressed on the gas, hoping to teach her a lesson. I rolled down my window and stuck out my head as the twenty-something-year-old looked back like she'd done nothing wrong.

"You stupid bitch!" I screamed as she and her children made it safely to the sidewalk. Realizing she'd dropped something, she darted back out into the street, causing me to come to a screeching halt, while the Range Rover drove away. Wanting to jump out of my car and whip her ass, I decided that it would be best to continue on with my mission.

The next bitch who runs in front of this car is going to get run the fuck over! I thought to myself as I pressed my foot on the gas, hoping to catch back up with them. Relieved that they hadn't gotten too far, and with only one car in between us, I soon caught back up. My impatience was building up as thoughts of running them off a cliff crept into my mind, yet I managed to stay focused. I followed them for an additional half an hour, before noticing the sign that indicated our final destination.

NICE CÔTE D'AZUR AIRPORT.

Where in the fuck are y'all going? I asked myself as they looked around for a parking space. Oblivious to the other cars that were all around me, I accidentally banged my rental into a parked Bentley.

Hard.

And it was then that we locked eyes.

Me and Oshyn.

She paused.

Never blinked.

Never got anyone else's attention to verify that it was me. She just stared at me with a look of delusion as I hopped out of the rental, leaving it behind for someone else to deal with. I had got it under an alias, anyway, and could've cared less what the consequences were. I had bigger problems.

My cover had been blown.

9

Chloe

"I need a ticket out of here right now!" I demanded like a lunatic.

In my outside voice.

The chick that was behind the counter at International Air looked at me like I was crazy. I'd caused an uproar, a scene I was sure that she wasn't used to. She probably hadn't seen a bitch like me other than in the movies.

This was Saint-Tropez.

Not the hood.

"I mean, do you speak fucking English?" I asked her as I slammed my fist on the counter that stood between us. She didn't have too long to answer, or her head would be slammed against the hard surface. I turned my head viciously from side to side, mimicking Linda

Blair in *The Exorcist,* as I tried finding someone capable of taking care of my request.

"What the fuck are y'all muthafuckas looking at?" I screamed at the crowd of white
tourists, who were just waiting to get home
from a relaxing weekend. No one dared to answer.

Oshyn, Brooklyn, and the children had already gone through security, and I wasn't sure
where they were going or what flight they
were taking, but if I had to take a guess, it was
Rochester. Tuff's funeral was in a few days,
and Brooklyn wouldn't miss that.

"Hello, miss. Can I help you with something?" asked a chunky man with a receding
hairline. He snapped me from my daze. "What
seems to be the problem?"

"What seems to be the problem?" I asked
rhetorically as I looked at his tag, which read
MANAGER, and was relieved that I would finally
be able to get the situation resolved. "The
problem is that I need an emergency flight
back to Rochester, New York, right now! There
was a death in the family, and my sister is on
the plane as we speak. We need to travel together!"

"I see," he said with his French accent, while
typing a few things into his computer.

With two fingers.

Moving as slow as a fucking turtle.

"Are you serious? Dude, can you *not* move
any faster than that?"

"Ma'am, I'm—"

"*Ma'am?* Do I fucking look like a ma'am to you? I'm twenty-eight years old. And if you don't hurry your fat ass up, you're going to have a serious problem on your hands!" I warned.

"I'm moving as fast as I can!" he replied with an attitude, never looking up to make eye contact. He typed a few more things, then stopped, before slowly lifting his head and looking at me. "I'm sorry, but that last flight to Rochester is sold out." He typed a little more. "The next flight I have doesn't leave until tomorrow afternoon. Would you like me to book that one for you?"

"If you don't get me out of here right now, I'm going to kill you!"

Acting like a four-year-old kid having a temper tantrum, I knocked all the brochures and advertisements off the counter and was ready to go to war when someone caught my eye.

He stood six foot four, with skin the color of black maple. I saw that his clothes were custom-made, and the snakeskin briefcase topped off my assumption.

He had plenty of money.

Maybe he was the one the old woman saw in my future?

Brushing off the idea, I diverted my attention back to the manager and was met by four security officers instead of a plane ticket.

"Ma'am, can you please come with us?" one

guy said, with an even thicker French accent than the manager's. He was the shortest one, standing five foot two, while all the taller men loomed over me.

"Fuck you, you little midget! And *hell no,* I can't go with you anywhere. He's *going* to get me a flight, and I'm *going* to get on that plane with my family, and you all are *going* to leave me the fuck alone!"

Steam rose from my head as I watched a crowd form around me and point their fingers in my direction. One of the bigger security officers grabbed my arm and yanked me up like I was a rag doll.

"You don't have a choice," he roared as he dragged me away from the counter. I swung at his face with the one hand that I had free and caught his jaw. He wrapped his huge biceps around my neck and put me in a headlock, dragging me away.

"I'm going to blow this bitch up!" I threatened, while gasping for air. "I'm coming back, and I'm going to kill all of you!"

I ended up all alone in what looked like an interrogation room, and for a moment I regretted not handling everything a little smoother. With all the commotion I'd attracted to myself, I was sure all chances of me catching up with Oshyn had been ruined. It would now take a miracle to change this situation around, yet I was still going to try to work my magic.

As I contemplated how I was going to get

myself out of this mess, the steel door opened and a strong muscleman who looked like a French version of Mike Tyson walked in.

"Hello. I'm the customs official and—"

"Did I ask you who the fuck you were?"

Unfazed by my interruption, he continued to talk with a voice that was much deeper and more masculine than Tyson's. "What are you doing here in this country? Are you on business? Vacation?"

"Yes . . . business," I answered.

Aggravated.

Pissed.

Ready to fight.

"What kind of business are you on without suitcases?" he asked. He then eyed the bathing suit that I still had on. "Odd attire to be traveling . . . yeah?"

"Fuck you," I spat sarcastically. "None of my information is any of your *fucking* business. That's what kind of business I'm on, and that's where my bags are!"

He gazed at me, not moved by my smart comebacks, then continued. "We have reason to believe that you are trying to smuggle drugs out of this country. We will execute a strip search to ensure that's not the case."

He smirked, revealing that he had already begun the search in his mind, and I played into it by opening and closing my legs just like Sharon Stone did in *Basic Instinct*. I'd managed to retie the sarong I had on around my body. Now it looked more like a little dress. I stood up and began to undress myself, taking everything off. Within seconds, I stood like a stripper preparing for the pole with nothing on and watched the print on his black uniform pants rise.

He was excited.

Really excited.

"I've been a really bad girl. Are you going to spank me?" I asked as I leaned over on the table, exposing my huge ass. I spread my legs and rubbed my hands along the crack of my butt, making sure to graze my fingers along my pussy.

And then I slapped my ass.

Really, really hard.

"Spank me, Daddy," I said seductively in a childlike voice. Those sick muthafuckas loved when you changed your voice to sound like an innocent child. Hopefully, all this bullshit would set me free. "Take out that big cock and stick it in my mouth to shut me the fuck up!"

I got up from my bending position and walked toward him. I dropped to my knees and reached for his zipper. The punk-ass customs officer, who had had so much to say a few minutes ago, was now speechless, knowing he was about to get his dick sucked. I managed to squeeze his big dick through the small slit of his pants and rubbed it against my face.

"What will you do for Mommy if I let you stick it down my throat and choke me with it?"

"What do you want Daddy to do for you?" he asked, playing along with my game. It was at that moment that I knew I had him.

"I want Daddy to get me on that flight so I can go home with my family." I licked the head of his peach stick and said, "I promise I'll be a good girl."

"Shut the fuck up, and show me how good you'll be," he ordered.

He put his hand on the back of my head and forced his dick even farther into my mouth, causing me to choke a bit. It had been a while since I'd given head, and my reflexes proved it. My jaw muscles clearly weren't what they used to be, because I gagged every time he thrust deeper into my mouth. Not one to complain, I took hold of the situation by wrapping my hand around his meat to slow down his movements.

And then I fondled it.

Tickled his balls.

I found my rhythm as my tongue swirled around his toy, making him flinch with every move I made. This head was going to get me on the plane. I knew it would.

It throbbed in my mouth, but it was worth it all. I could tell my freedom was just minutes away by the way his head tilted backward and his pupils rolled to the back of his head, leaving only the color white. Besides, his long, hard throbs let me know that he was about to explode any second. I pulled and yanked at it, causing a suction effect in my mouth. It was my time to shine. My time to break free. He moaned, squirmed a little, and with no ability to contain himself, he released his warm, creamy island babies all over my face. I wiped some of his nut off my eye and stuck it in my mouth for an added touch.

"Was I a good girl?" I asked, while licking the rest of his cum off my mouth.

"Stand up," he demanded. He tucked his satisfied dick back into his pants and zipped swiftly.

"So now . . . I need to get on that flight. Are you letting me go?"

"I said get up!" he shouted, as his boss could be heard outside the door.

The tone of his voice confused me.

It was harsh and authoritative. I stood up, with his creamy juice still attached to my face, and looked at him. He turned me around forcefully, slapped some handcuffs on me, and proceeded to say, "You're under arrest for the assault of a customs officer!"

10

Oshyn

"I saw her," I kept telling Brooklyn fearfully. He had just gotten comfortable in his seat and had closed his eyes. "I saw Chloe in the parking lot. Here at the airport, just as we were parking!"

"Oshyn, please, not now. Not right now!"

He rubbed his temples, trying to relieve whatever stress I was causing him. If he rubbed any harder, he would take the black off of his skin. I had wanted to tell him about seeing Chloe when I first noticed her, but my lips wouldn't move. The lady crossing the street carelessly with her children had had me spellbound. The thought of hitting those children was too much to bear. And as much as I hated to admit it, it had seemed like my dead son was one of the children with her. I'd been frozen in place, wondering if my mind was playing tricks on me.

I stared at Brooklyn as his eyes remained closed. I knew he was frustrated. He grieved for both me and Tuff but was probably sick of me. The plane had yet to take off, and he wasn't too fond of the sky, so I was sure he wanted to go to sleep before we took off. I knew he would never believe me, I thought to myself.

"Baby . . . please, wake up for just a minute."

I nudged him softly on his arm, and he shifted, trying to get me off of him. I knew my antics were becoming annoying, but crazy or not, I saw what I saw.

"What? What is it? Talk," Brooklyn finally said.

He sat his seat up, even though he wasn't supposed to have it down, anyway, and looked in my eyes. He didn't have to say it. The sarcasm, anger, and disappointment were written all over his face.

"Ladies and gentlemen, due to the weather, we have a slight delay in our initial takeoff. Please be patient. We'll be departing as soon as possible. Thank you for flying with International Air," one of the stewardesses announced.

"Don't stop talking now," he threatened, obviously beyond frustrated.

I shifted in my seat, regretting the fact that

I had even brought this up, but I knew it needed to be discussed.

"Brooklyn, I know I've been acting a little crazy lately, but—"

"Please, I can't. My head hurts," he confessed, rubbing it again. "My mind . . . hurts. I can't take this crap right now, Oshyn!"

I gave him a stern look. "Crap?"

Right before I was getting ready to dig into his ass about how he was speaking to me, he reached into his pocket and handed me a bottle of pills. Oddly, they had been prescribed to me, and I hadn't been to a doctor in months.

"Zoloft?" I asked, snatching the bottle out of his hand. "What are you doing with this?"

"Take them!" He snatched the bottle out of my hand, then proceeded to open it. He tilted the bottle, and two pills fell into his palm. "Please . . . take them!"

"Fuck you, Brooklyn!" I said through clenched teeth as I unfastened my seat belt to sit with Bella and Mye, who were sitting across from us. I quickly took Mye out of Bella's lap and sat down in the empty seat next to her, then made myself comfortable. From her heavy sigh, it was obvious that I was bothering her, but I could care less.

"What the hell is wrong with you?" I asked her as I put Mye back to sleep.

"Nothin'," she replied as she rocked her

head to whatever music was playing in her earphones.

"Yeah, it had better be nothing."

I rolled my eyes.

Daring her to say something. Anything. But she wouldn't.

"Bella, hand me some tissue from out of your purse," I said, trying to dig green stuff out of Mye's nose with my fingernail, but those monsters wouldn't budge. I turned back to Bella, who had her eyes closed, and saw that she was still rocking to whatever beat played in her head.

I was sure that she heard me but didn't feel like arguing anymore. Not wanting to cause any drama on the plane, I bent down and stuck my hand up under her seat to grab her small hot pink Juicy bag. I sat it on my lap and unzipped it, only to find a condom sitting on top of all her mess. Without thinking twice, I yanked her earphones out of her ears.

"What the fuck is this?" I held the package up to her face and waited for an explanation. I could care less who heard my foul language at that point.

"Why were you going through my stuff?" she asked, totally disregarding the fact that her nine-year-old ass had been caught red-handed with a fucking condom.

I held Mye close to my chest as I took my right hand and wrapped it around her neck, of course, doing my best to squeeze the life out of her as quietly as I could before anyone could stop me.

"Oshyn, what are you doing?" Brooklyn asked as he rushed to pry my hand off of Bella.

I never noticed him get up. Never even noticed his huge frame standing over me.

Bella coughed violently and gasped for air.

"She's having sex, Brooklyn!" I held up the condom for him to see, while he managed to take Mye out of my hands.

"Shhhh! You're making too much noise!" said someone a few rows back.

I ignored them. Never even looked back to see who'd said it. Was handling family business, and that took priority. We were only four rows from the back, so there weren't many people around us.

"But you tried to kill her," Brooklyn whispered sadly.

"She's nine years old, and she's having sex!" I yelled. "Do something about it! Oh, wait . . . since she's not your daughter, you don't have to reprimand her, is that it?"

"Lower your voice," he warned.

I peered over the seat and realized that we had attracted some unwanted attention from the nosy people that sat around us.

"Don't *nobody* give a fuck about these people! Fuck you *and* fuck them!"

"Handle your problems at home, lady. This is a public place," someone in front of me yelled.

"The very next person who decides to say anything to me or my family will get dealt with," I warned.

Another woman joined in on the attack against me, and just when I was about to go off on her, I noticed someone getting on the plane. Although we were sitting at the back of the huge airbus, I was still able to get a glimpse of who it was.

"Chloe?" I said out loud to no one in particular. The mouths of the passengers were still moving, but I didn't notice anything. Just watched as the woman I saw in the parking lot took a seat in first class. "She's here. Chloe's on the plane!" I whispered to Brooklyn. Instantly, my body began to shiver, and goose bumps popped up all over my arms. "I gotta get off of here!" I shouted.

"I'm sorry, but is there a problem over here?" the stewardess asked, blocking the view of my sister.

"Brooklyn, she's here. She's on the plane!" I screamed even louder.

I needed him to respond.

Needed him to take me seriously.

To say anything other than the loud screams of nothing that escaped from his mouth.

"No, there's nothing going on here," Brooklyn told the stewardess calmly. "My wife was just about to take her medication. She gets like this right before flying," he lied.

Brooklyn tried to spare himself the embarrassment of telling her the truth, that his wife was going insane and there was nothing he could do about it. I ignored him and began devising a plan to make my way up to the front. I had to see for myself if it was really her or not.

"Both of you move out of my way. I'm going to see my sister." As I proceeded to get up out of my seat, with the intent of walking forward, I was blocked by Brooklyn's chest. "Move!"

"Sit down," he warned.

"Get . . . out . . . of . . . my . . . way!" I demanded.

He took his hand and threw me back in my seat like I was a child. Like I was one of his children. Like I couldn't make my own decisions. I heard a few cheers from the crowd, then turned to give them all dirty looks.

"I will put both of you off the plane if she doesn't calm down, sir," the stewardess informed Brooklyn. She was obviously at her wit's end, and even though I could tell she didn't want to be, I was leaving her no choice but to be stern.

Brooklyn spoke with fire in his voice. "Don't worry. It won't happen again. I have it all under con—"

"Fuck you, bitch! You're just trying to keep me away from my sister, just like everyone else. But you won't succeed this time. I will kill

101

you before I let you keep me from her. I'll kill you!" I screamed.

"That's it," the stewardess declared, right before walking to the front of the plane. "I'm not putting up with this anymore. She's out of here."

11

Chloe

When I was several feet over the threshold of the plane, a sigh of relief filled my senses. It seemed as if every passenger awaited my arrival. Here I had been in trouble, had just sucked a crusty dick, and I still got the red carpet treatment. The anorexic-looking stewardess moved swiftly, telling me the only space for my oversize pocketbook was in the open compartment where she stood. I felt like I had no choice as I heard the captain announce that we were now ready to depart.

"You're in seat three A," the stewardess announced with her French accent.

I chuckled. "Ain't this a bitch? First class. Humph, I'm the shit," I boasted to myself.

I shot the skinny white bitch a grin and threw my pocketbook in the air to store it up top. When it was midair, I realized how much other luggage was in the compartment, and I struggled for a second to squeeze mine in. That was until a tall gentleman stood up to assist me.

I froze.

It must've been fate.

It was the same guy I'd seen brush past me when I was fussing to get on the plane. As he moved my way, I got a whiff of his good-smelling cologne, glanced at his tall, slender frame and attractive bald head. It was shiny, sexy, and simply needed me to rub it for perfection.

There were only about five other people in first class, so I held my composure and just nodded my thanks when he touched my hand to help. My first thought was, *Damn, this is it!*

He's the one.

All six foot four of him.

Luck was surely on my side for the day. First, I had managed to talk my way out of being put in jail by threatening the customs guy that I would tell his boss the truth. I told that idiot that I'd held some of his semen in my mouth and spit it into my bra for evidence. His faggot ass believed me and agreed to get me on the plane if I kept my mouth shut. Secondly, meeting Mr. Right on the plane, and realizing he was in seat 3C, was just like hitting the lottery.

As soon as I sat down, chills flew through

my body. His smell mesmerized me to the point that I was afraid to look him in the face. I couldn't help but think back to the old lady. She'd said that he was tall and dark, with plenty of money. My fellow passenger was definitely tall and slender, and he reminded me of Michael Jordan, just a few shades darker. He was sexy, well kept, and dressed like he was making some serious paper. He asked me if I had enough space, because he would move to another seat nearby if I wanted to stretch out.

"Oh no, I'm fine," I said with ease. On the real, I wanted to jump over into his seat and jam my tongue down his throat.

It was official. I was smitten like a schoolgirl being manipulated by an older man. He was flipping through a *Black Enterprise* magazine, while I eyed him like a correctional officer watching an inmate. His twenty-thousand-dollar Cartier watch had me captivated. It was an edition that had been featured in *Forbes,* all blinged out, and that Tommy had told me about. Personally, I'd never had the pleasure of experiencing anything special edition for my wrist, yet I made a mental note to get his and hers soon.

It had my nipples cold and hard, wondering how many carats sat around the diamond-encrusted bezel. Then there was the one diamond stud in his left ear. It had to be three carats, a VVS stone, I was sure.

I wanted him.

Badly.

I was willing to do anything.

The two-by-two bathroom was fine.

The seat that we sat in would be better.

My eyes seemed to dart away every time he caught me looking at him. As soon as I felt the plane ascending into the air, I lifted my window shade to take a look at the clouds. It was my hope that the serene scene would take my mind off Jordan's twin. But within seconds, he sucked me in even more.

With his Northern accent, he started and wouldn't stop. "So, was your trip business or pleasure?"

I tried to speak . . . just couldn't. I was tongue-tied and kept my eyes on his bright white teeth. "Ahhhhhh . . ."

He smiled even more. "Are you thinking about your man or something?" he asked.

I knew the accent was Jersey or New York, so I thought of something to say. "I'm single but used to date a guy from Jersey. That's where you're from, right?"

"Nah, Manhattan, actually," he corrected, showing me every dimple he had.

"So, tell me, what do you do?" I asked him suspiciously.

"A little of this and that." He paused. "And you?"

"Big things. Things you could never imagine." I smiled.

"Word."

He crossed his legs, letting his crisp pant leg drape over his gators. Everything he wore appeared to be top-notch, even the custom-made button-down shirt with the initials C.M.

"So, what's C.M. stand for?"

He extended his hand. "Pardon my manners. Carlos Manning," he said. "And you are?"

"Chloe." I paused. I thought about saying Chloe Manning but wasn't sure if he'd appreciate the humor. "Chloe Rodriguez," I finally said, then smiled.

"Well, Chloe Rodriguez, tell me a little about yourself. We've got a long ride." He rested his head back on the seat. "I would ask how your day was, but I would say that it's safe to say you spent your time swimming." And then he laughed.

"Cute. Real cute," I replied, returning his humorous gesture. His eyes, which roamed up and down my body, let me know that he was referring to my bathing suit. Something that was totally inappropriate for this type of travel. "I was in a rush. Didn't have time to change."

Just then the commotion at the back of the plane started again. It was the same annoying commotion that had been going on when I first got on the plane. My lust for Carlos had sidetracked me then, but the shit was getting louder.

All of a sudden, a chubby, dark-skinned stewardess brushed Carlos as she came bolting down the aisle. She rushed over to Miss Anorexia, complaining. "I got her name. Oshyn Jones," she said, reading from a small piece of ripped paper. "She's traveling with two kids and her husband," she snapped. "He's trying to calm her down, and it's not working, if you ask me." She paused, placing her hands on her hips, and gave a huge huff. "What should I do?"

"I mean, we're about to depart. What can you do now?" Miss Anorexia said, rolling her eyes. "I don't like dealing with that now. I wanna get in the air. Let's just leave it alone. I'm sure her husband will be able to calm her down."

I couldn't help but wonder what kind of scene Oshyn was making that was causing this kind of uproar. She was normally the one to remain calm, but everyone seemed to be aggravated by her presence. Maybe she told Brooklyn about seeing me in the parking lot, I thought to myself. Maybe she saw me get on the plane.

Abruptly, I cleared my throat. "Excuse me . . . but as a paying passenger, it's annoying," I interjected.

Carlos took charge. "Just close the curtains. That should do the trick," he said with confidence.

My thought was to talk shit and press the situation hard with tons of complaints. But I didn't want to buck Carlos. His smoothness had everyone in awe, even had both stewardesses eating from the palm of his hand. The heavyset one closed the curtain separating first class from coach, while I thought about my next malicious comment.

"Where's the plane marshal? I mean . . . or at least a confined compartment for people like that?" My hands were spread apart, and my temper had risen, as I'd almost forgot Carlos was watching me. "Damn! I paid a lot of money for this first-class seat. And there's no class at all on this plane!"

I stopped.

Caught myself.

I was back to the real Chloe.

Carlos looked at me with surprise. "So, you're a naughty girl, huh?"

"No, not really. I'm so sorry," I pleaded. "I just hate chaos, and that passenger shouting and acting crazy is getting to me." I paused to put my puppy dog face on. "You see, mental illness runs in my family."

"Word," he said sympathetically.

Instantly I got wet. His concerned voice, mixed with the roughness of how he spoke, turned me on. He had class, yet he had a ruggedness to him. "At least three people in my family died at the hands of mental illness."

"So sorry to hear that, but the good thing is you're fine. And I do mean fine." He grinned.

"So, how old are you?" I asked curiously.

"How old do I look?" he shot back.

I melted into the seat as he made love to me with his eyes. "Uhhh, twenty-eight?"

"Thirty-one," he admitted.

"You look good."

"Not as good as you," he said, licking his supple lips. Without warning, he moved over to the empty middle seat between us. "Mind if I get a little closer?" Carlos asked.

I simply beamed, then spread my legs. "I like a man who takes charge."

Carlos looked shocked.

And I wanted to remain a lady so we could start our relationship the right way. I decided to take things slow, so I grabbed his oversize hand that held the large diamond and placed it directly under my sarong. His hand felt warm, soothing, almost as if it belonged on my pussy.

And had found its home.

He knew what I wanted.

The question was, could he give it to me without anyone noticing? Hell, we had an eight-hour flight back to the States. I imagined I would cum three or four times during that time.

12

Chloe

At the hotel.

Getting fucked.

Tuff's funeral wasn't for another two days, so I had some time to spare until I had to get down to business. There was no rush, since Brooklyn and Oshyn weren't going to leave town until his cousin was buried. I had time to have a little fun. Fun I deserved.

"The real Chloe is back," I told myself, puffing on a woo given to me by Carlos. To my surprise, it was a blunt mixed with weed and cocaine. I had never smoked a woo before. Guess the hospital kept me from being up on things. Oddly, it calmed my nerves and helped me focus on his slick ass. Hell, he was hitting me with all kinds of surprises. The nigga was into everything I thought he wouldn't be into.

His business attire and confident swagger had me fooled. Everything about Carlos was now starting to surprise me.

When I first met him on the plane, his demeanor told me he was stuck up, suave, and debonair. Instead, I'd hooked up and fallen in love with an undercover thug. He dressed the part of a businessman daily, but on the real, the nigga was hood. Of course, I liked it like that. Hood mixed with plenty of money. *What could be better?* I asked myself, with my legs spread wide open on the king-size bed.

Carlos stood above me, caressing my bare thighs and throwing out words that got me horny again. "You want some more of big Dick Willie," he taunted, grabbing his shit.

"C'mere, Los," I called over to him.

He turned his back and slipped on his crisp slacks, letting me know our fuck fest had to stop. We had already pounded our way through three rounds of sex, yet my pussy continued to pulsate, telling me it wanted more of Carlos. Everything about him felt right: the way he talked, the way he moved, and the way he handled his business on the phone. I felt like yanking Carlos by his tie back onto the bed, but I knew he had to go. His big show would start at nine tonight, and the artist was expected to arrive for a sound check at three o'clock.

"So, what time you coming to my show?" he

asked, rushing over to me and bending down to kiss my sweet pussy.

I lay back on the bed with my head resting against the headboard, unable to answer. I simply moaned, closed my eyes, and let his wet lips make love to my clit.

Abruptly, he stopped, but I yanked his bald head back toward the treasure.

"Come here," I begged. "Eat it, pleaseee. Just one more time."

"I can't, Chloe." He laughed slightly. "Tonight I got you after the show. I gotta go meet up with the sound company. They need their paper." He kissed at me through the air. "You know I got a lot of money riding on this show."

All I heard was blah, blah, blah. I was used to getting everything my way, and I wanted him *now*.

"So, what's in it for me?" I asked, pulling him by the collar. I lifted my body and pushed myself toward him. We met eye to eye, with Carlos still on his feet, leaning my way.

"Yo, tonight I'll bring the profits back to the hotel room, and we'll fuck all night."

I got excited.

"On top of the money, right?" I asked excitedly.

I loosened my grip, noticing Carlos squirming to get away.

"Word is bond."

"And we upgrading to a suite tonight, right?"

"No doubt," he said with confidence. "Anything you want, you get."

I smiled widely inside and damn near came. Those words were music to my ears.

"I'll be there by ten. I got front row seats, right?" I asked as he slipped his pistol into a cuff underneath the bottom of his pant leg.

He grinned. "Only the best for my lady," he uttered, walking toward the hotel door.

I smiled back, wondering how the hell I had landed his chocolate ass. "Love you!" I shouted.

The door slammed, and I rolled over like a dog in heat, thinking about how my life was about to change. I knew I would soon be a housewife, so I had to change up my wardrobe. A few presentable pieces wouldn't hurt, just in case he needed me to accompany him on business. I needed to get my hair done, and most importantly, I needed to get on the Internet in the lobby to find us a place to live when we returned to Manhattan.

Carlos traveled a lot, but it would be my job to make our home comfy and cozy for his return. He told me that three to four times per month he left the city to make his bread. Doing shows was his only livelihood. It was how he made his millions ... a gracious living. From what he'd revealed, he'd been mixed up in some illegal moneymaking shit a few years back where he made a lot of cash, and this pretty much gave him start-up money to become a big-time promoter.

That was where the whole gun thing came in. He needed it. Said some folks were after him. Wanted to see him dead. I wasn't worried, because Carlos was about his word. Plus, he'd told me a few stories about things he'd done in the past. People he'd shot. Dudes he'd stabbed. And haters he'd disposed of. The thought of my man sent chills up and down my spine. Then the interruption came.

It was him.

My supplemental check.

Old-ass Tommy.

"Yes!" I answered like a raging bull on the second ring.

"Chloe, I've been calling you." Tommy sounded like a weak lamb.

"Oh really," I countered, showing that I didn't give a fuck.

He sighed heavily. "You got the money I sent on Tuesday?"

"Yeah, I got it." I smacked my lips and remained silent, hoping he would get angry and hang up.

His next words sent me into oblivion.

"I need to see you soon. I'll even come to Rochester," he uttered. "I . . . I . . . I changed my will like we discussed." He paused hesitantly. "But I need to see you before I turn it in to my lawyer. There are a few important things we gotta discuss."

My eyeballs rolled to the back of my head, and dollar signs replaced my brown pupils. I couldn't speak. Could barely even move. How honored. Tommy wanted me to now be the beneficiary of the majority of his belongings. His estate, which we had already discussed back in the hospital, was worth more than three million dollars. It would be a stretch having him come to Rochester, but I had no other choice.

"Chloe, are you there?" he asked worriedly.

"I'm here."

"I know you're there for your brother's funeral, so stay put. I'm coming there. The will has to be changed immediately."

I sensed the urgency in his voice. His voice was a bit weaker than before. Sounded like death was knocking on his door a lot faster than we both had anticipated. I braced myself to act concerned for the first time.

"Is everything okay?"

"Not really. I'll explain when I get there. I'll call with our meeting spot when I get off the plane. I'll have to come right back, so we'll meet near the airport."

"Bet," I said, then hung up to fabricate my plan.

At ten o'clock sharp, I found myself in the green room backstage, rubbing elbows with the elite. The room was small, intimate, and laced with two tables carrying the finest wines, fruits, bottles of liquor, and at the headliner's request, Rémy Martin VSOP. I stood in the corner, watching Ludacris's manager shout the dos and don'ts of how things were to go down, but my man handled it all. He was sharp with his words, even though the sweat could be seen across his forehead.

Suddenly nasty thoughts entered my mind as I watched Carlos give instructions to a few more of his workers. "I need it done right," I heard him say, then saw two chicks in the corner snicker his way.

Before I knew it, I'd gotten closer to them. They were two of ten people in the lowly lit room, and they laughed secretively in the corner, as if they were making comments about us all. The music played low inside, sounding as if it was coming from a hidden iPod, but it didn't keep me from hearing the word *flunky*.

They both turned as I got up on them. The dominant, mouthy-looking bitch just glared when I asked if the champagne had arrived yet.

"I'm not sure," she responded after giving me a dirty look. "And you are?"

"Oh, I'm none of your fucking business." I extended my hand. "I'm with my fiancé. Just making sure everything is okay."

They both looked at me like I was stuck on stupid.

"Carlos," I announced. "I'm with Carlos."

They burst into laughter.

"Well, I'm Sheila, and this is Tyese. We're with D-Rock. He's opening for Luda. And, honey, we know all about Carlos." They laughed again.

Sheila had on a short, strapless leather dress, three-inch stilettos, and a bad weave all down her back. It was clear she thought she was hot shit by the way she flipped me off with her eyes. Her girl paid more attention to my expression and knew I wasn't to be fucked with.

I folded my arms tightly across my torso and told them that I thought I'd overheard them saying something about my man.

"I just want to be clear. If something is said about him, say it to me." I was firm with my tone, but quiet enough to keep our bitter conversation under wraps.

"You don't know, do you?" Sheila asked innocently.

"Know what?" I asked. My expression puzzled them both, but I refused to let them know they had caught me off guard. So I just hit them with confident words that most kept-in-the-dark women spoke. "I know all that I need to know."

"Oh, I'm sure," Sheila mocked, flipping her weave in the process.

The song "Stand by Your Man" played in my mind. *Fuck these haters,* I told myself as the MC for the show was heard throughout the arena. At the same time my phone rang.

I felt trapped.

It was Tommy.

Didn't want to leave, but that money was calling. The D-Rock bitches shook their heads sympathetically as they watched me talk in codes, then turn to leave the room.

"Nice meeting you," Sheila stated in a mocking tone.

"Oh, I'll be back. And you will see me again." I hit her with a fake smile and jetted out of the green room, hoping Carlos wouldn't notice that I was gone. I knew I had less than an hour to make it back. I figured the show would be going on and he wouldn't miss me, anyway.

As soon as I stepped into the revolving door of the Hilton by the airport fifteen minutes later, my adrenaline was in overdrive. The lobby was full of people quickly moving back and forth. For ten thirty at night it was busier than I'd expected. I kept looking around for Tommy and even checked the bar. Finally, I noticed him sitting alone near the fireplace in the lobby. The area he'd chosen was cozy, with two comfy high-back chairs, and a stool and table placed neatly in between.

"Hey, Tommy," I said excitedly, walking up on him.

He could barely turn his stiff neck as he greeted me in a depressed tone.

His situation was serious. I could feel it. He looked even older than before. Almost fragile. Like two minutes from his deathbed.

"You feeling okay?" I asked.

Tommy cleared his throat, then coughed. "Not really," he revealed, then coughed again, like he suffered from a bad case of emphysema, the smoker's disease. "Look, I'll go into details later." He stopped to take a deep breath. "My daughter is coming to town tomorrow, and I wanted to get this business straight with you."

My face was already balled up before he could finish his sentence. "Your daughter? I thought you said she didn't want you in her life. You said you hadn't seen her in ten years."

"I hadn't, Chloe. But she called. And honestly, I'm not doing well. So I wanted you to have a copy of my will. You know how things go when people die." He paused, then looked at me like he loved me for real. "My daughter is my blood. She'll get everything by law if you don't sign these papers."

Judging by the way Tommy pulled the papers from the large brown envelope, I knew I'd be a multimillionaire soon. He moved like he was one hundred years old as he flipped through the stack. His hands seemed to be peeling and were wrinkled, but I rubbed them, anyway, before going into my purse.

"How's your daughter?" he asked me out of the blue. Luckily, he didn't look me in the face. He was busy trying to find the spots where I needed to sign.

"Oh, she's getting better. Thanks to you." I smiled.

I pulled out one of Carlos's Black & Milds and kicked my foot up on the stool. I just shook my head back and forth as I lit up. I couldn't believe how Tommy was deteriorating.

He needed a coffin to rest in.

Bad.

I got so caught up staring that I didn't hear him rushing me for a signature. He said he wanted to hurry so he could catch the last flight out, at 11:25 to be exact. I wanted him gone, too. He coughed uncontrollably, trying to get his next words out.

"Chloe, sign here for now. I'll get you copies as soon as I turn this in to my lawyer. I think we should move in together when you get back."

I swallowed hard. "Just give me time to get my daughter straight." Then I stood, kissed him on the cheek, and told him I loved him.

"I love you, too, Chloe. Just know you're the best thing that ever happened to me." He stopped to cough again. "I'll call you tomorrow. I gotta catch this flight."

Hell, I gotta get back to my man, I told myself. *The bitches are probably all over him by now.* I rushed out of the hotel, doing thirty with my feet.

13

Chloe

Knock . . . knock . . . knock!

"Who is it?" Carlos screamed at the unwanted visitor who was pounding on our hotel
room door. Although it was going on ten
o'clock in the morning, we had just fallen
asleep after counting all the money *we* had
made at the show last night. The sun was no
match for the blinds, as not a speck of light
peeked into the room. It was dark as night in
here.

"Room service," the irritated female voice
said with a deep Spanish accent. She had a job
to do, and we were messing up her flow, or my
guess was she had seen some nice pieces she
wanted to steal and we had gotten in the way
of her plans. Either way, she was out of luck.

"Go away!" Carlos demanded as he turned

over to face me. He took his hands and pulled me closer to his naked chocolate brown body, and then he kissed me on my forehead right before drifting back off to sleep. I closed my eyes in an attempt to follow in his steps, but there was no way I could do the same.

I still couldn't get the hundreds of thousands of dollars, which took us hours to count, out of my mind. I could still smell the sweet scent of currency, so much of it that it made me sick. So much dirty money that my fingertips had turned dingy. So much of it that I was never going to let this dude get away, because this was different. He trusted me. Never once thinking that I would set him up. And for the first time in my life, the thought never crossed my mind.

I was used to getting money. Big money. Long money. I had traveled all around the world in private jets and on custom yachts, but nothing compared to this. Simple and pure love. The great sex we had and the chemistry that we shared made all this money an added bonus. I couldn't figure out what had gotten into me, but this love thing was a feeling that I could learn to get used to.

Now I had to choose between Carlos and Brooklyn, a choice that would disappoint one of them deeply if it wasn't him, but I decided to worry about that later. Carlos was here, in the flesh, with his arms wrapped around me. Feeling safe, I dozed off.

* * *

"Babe," I heard a voice say as I felt a soft tug on my shoulder. "Baby, are you going to sleep all day? Wake up!"

The tug got a little harder.

Turned into shoves.

I peeked my head out of the fluffy white comforter, only to be greeted by the scent of eggs, bacon, and grits, and then I realized that Carlos was no longer lying by my side.

"What time is it?" I asked, not really wanting to be bothered. It felt like I had been asleep for only a few minutes, and I had no intention of waking up. I was extremely tired.

"It's almost one o'clock. . . . Wake up!" Carlos said as he snatched the cover off of me. I got an immediate attitude and snatched it back, placing it over my body, where it was originally. "I brought you breakfast in bed, so you need to get up and eat it."

My stomach growled, and my bladder felt like it was going to burst, but I was too exhausted to move. I felt like if I could just go back to sleep, I wouldn't feel the hunger pains, and the explosion of my bladder would just be an afterthought. So I closed my eyes and tried to ignore his constant words, but none of it seemed to work.

"Chloe, wake your ass up!" Carlos shouted.

I opened my eyes just enough to watch him walk over to the window and pull the curtains open, letting the incredibly bright sunlight in.

I nestled back under the covers like a vampire, trying to avoid being burnt to dust.

"Are you serious? Why can't you just leave me alone?" I pleaded with him.

"Because you can sleep when you're dead, that's why. If you're going to be with me, you'll learn quickly that sleep is not a luxury that we can afford. I barely sleep. There is just too much money to make. Too much money to spend."

Now he was talking my language.

He pulled the cover off of me again, and this time I let him, exposing my bare body against the crisp white sheets. It took my eyes a while to adjust to the daylight as I reached over and grabbed a piece of crunchy bacon from off the plate.

"I'm up now!" I announced with an attitude as I took a bite of the meat. "What do you have planned for the day?"

He was already fully dressed in a pair of Hugo Boss jeans and a red Lacoste polo. He grabbed the suitcase full of money and put it on the bed, unzipped it, and took bundles of money out of it, spreading it all over my body.

He took his hands and pried my legs apart, exposing my thick pink pussy. My nipples stood firmly up and pointed in his direction, letting him know that they were ready to be sucked on. Letting him know that I was ready to be sucked on.

I swallowed the last piece of bacon as he

kissed my treasure. The urge that I had to pee was quickly replaced with the urge I had to nut all over his face. Then, without warning, he slid the tip of his tongue directly into my asshole, making me jump. Making me cum before I wanted to. It felt so good that I couldn't hold it in any longer.

"Wow, that was fast," he said as he saw the flow of happiness that seemed to pour nonstop out of my pussy. He smiled at me with the happy juice glazed over his face, and with ass juice glazed over his tongue.

Yeah, this is going to work out great, I thought as he went to the bathroom to clean himself off. What I loved more than anything else was a nasty nigga, and I had one in my possession. I finished up the breakfast, which had turned cold, swallowing the last piece of egg when he came out of the bathroom.

He got a little closer and touched my hair with his fingertips, and as he worked his way down to my ear, I jumped. I moved his hand and turned my head away before he had the opportunity to notice that one of my ears was fake.

"Why don't you like when I touch you there?" he asked, noticing that this wasn't the first time that I had moved his hand.

"My ears are sensitive," I lied. "Never really liked anyone playing around them." Just like a man, he shrugged his shoulders and dismissed my pet peeve.

"You never even told me what happened to your face."

I didn't know what to say. Just ignored him until he continued.

"Well, get up and get dressed," he said to me as he began putting the money back into the suitcase. "We're going to Toronto today. I want to do some shopping, maybe even hit up some casinos."

As tempting as that sounded, my focus immediately went to Oshyn. She was the real reason that I was even in the city, and I didn't want to lose sight of that fact. I was never one to let a man take me off my game, but with Carlos, I was making an exception. Just as I was about to tell him that I couldn't go with him, I quickly remembered the fact that Oshyn had come for the funeral, too, and wouldn't leave until her husband's cousin was buried. So, if nothing else, that bought me some time. Toronto was only a two-hour trip from Rochester, so I could make it back in no time. I got up and got dressed like I was told.

The two-hour drive flew by quicker than I thought it would, and it was a little after three in the afternoon when we reached our destination. Toronto, Canada. I hadn't been there since I left Rochester and moved to Raleigh, but it was still beautiful. An exact replica of

Manhattan, New York, with all the five-star restaurants and hotels to match.

"Where do you want to go first?" he asked, letting me know that the ball was in my court. That today was my day. That every day would always be my day.

"Put Bloor Street West in the navigation system," I instructed him. "That's where I want to go first."

This was one of Toronto's Fifth Avenue and Rodeo Drive look-alike streets, which housed some of the most expensive boutiques. It took us only about ten minutes to get there from where we were, and I immediately got excited, like a child on Christmas Day. It had been way too long since money was at my disposal, and I just couldn't contain myself. I started to hyperventilate.

"There! There! Pull over there!" I demanded. Once I laid my eyes on the Hermès boutique, all my worries went away. I practically hopped out of the car before it stopped rolling, and Carlos took care of the valet dude. When all of that was settled, he grabbed my hand and led me through the doorway of pure heaven.

"Good afternoon," an older woman said to me with a French accent. I had forgot that in Canada they spoke French, but then again, I thought to myself, *Who the fuck cares?* Her jet-black hair had a single white strip in the middle, and she wore a nicely tailored black suit. Probably St. John. She was very polished.

"Hey," I replied as I brushed past her to get my hands on one of the bags. I didn't really want to entertain small talk. My goal was to just get in and get out as fast as I could so that we could get back to Rochester. Trying to mix business with pleasure.

Carlos followed behind me like a lost puppy as I bounced from counter to counter, trying to see which bag I wanted to take home. They all seemed to reach out for me, begging me to take them. And then I spotted it. The one that caught my attention and never let it go.

"That one," I said to the woman, pointing her in the direction of the bag I was talking about.

She took a long glance at the bag I was referring to and then at me. "Ummm, yes. That particular style is sixty-five thousand dollars. Perhaps I can show you where our five-thousand-dollar Hermès bags are."

It seemed like time stood still as I felt the anger in me slowly rise to the top, like lava in a volcano, ready to erupt at any second. I took a moment to reevaluate what I looked like and determine what had made her say that bullshit to me. My jeans were Rock & Republic, and I had on a short-sleeve silk Alice and Olivia blouse. A pair of Tory Burch flats adorned my feet, and my hair was bouncy and in perfect place. No diamonds dripped off my ears, my neck, my wrists, or my fingers, like they had once before, but I was going to make sure that that would never happen again. The jewelry store would be our next stop. I couldn't afford to be mistaken for an average bitch again.

"Come. Let me show you where they are," the saleslady insisted as she unknowingly knocked me out of my daydream and back into reality.

"You dumb bitch, I know exactly what I said! Take the fucking bag that I asked you for down now!" I snapped.

I startled her.

Could tell by the way she paused that she was frozen in fear.

I had opened my mouth to let her have some more when I felt Carlos's warm touch on my shoulder, letting me know that he would handle the rest.

It reminded me of the *Pretty Woman* movie, where Richard Gere took control.

"I'm sure you just misheard her," Carlos told the lady, giving her the benefit of the doubt. "She said that she wanted to see *this* bag, not the cheap ones that you're trying to lead her to."

"Oh, okay . . . y-yeah. I m-mean yes, of course," she stuttered as she scuffled back to the item I had originally requested.

She took the black crocodile-skin Birkin bag out of the case and handed it to me. The hardware was plated in fourteen-karat gold, and this particular bag had diamonds encrusted on the buckle.

"I want this," I told her.

Carlos took stacks of hundreds out of his bag and sat them on the table. The amount of money equaled the cost of the bag plus the tax, but we got a bit of a discount since our money was worth more over here than it was in the States. The saleslady was preparing to wrap up the bag, but I let her know that I would be carrying it out as is.

"But of course, Mrs. . . . . Mrs. . . . . I'm sorry. I didn't get your name," she admitted as we began to walk away.

"Fuck off, bitch," were the last words she heard me say as we left the building.

"Damn, my baby is expensive," Carlos said as he took a closer look at his sixty-five-thousand-dollar investment. "I need to start making more money to be with you," he joked.

And he was right.

This was just the beginning.

"Where to next?" he asked, allowing me to lead the way, and I knew just the spot, a diamond boutique that would make Elizabeth Taylor proud, Royal de Versailles.

We didn't have to walk far, because it was right next door to Hermès, and when we entered, we were greeted with nothing but smiles. *Must be the bag,* I concluded, as everyone had a hard time keeping their eyes off of it.

"You have impeccable taste," a guy sitting behind the counter said to me.

"Thank you," I said back, finally glad that someone was able to appreciate class when they saw it.

"You're a diamond girl," he continued, laying the flattery on as thick as he could. I assumed that he had been doing this for a while, or he knew a bad bitch when he saw one. Either way his words were music to my ears.

"I need it all," I confessed. "Earrings, bracelet . . ."

"And what about a ring?" he said, directing that question to Carlos.

I assumed that he would stutter at the sight of pressure, but Carlos proved me wrong by just smiling and smoothly saying, "Whatever she wants."

I had found my big poppa!

The jeweler had me try on all the flawless pieces, and at least an hour went by before I found the right ones. A six-carat pair of diamond earrings hung off my ears, while a five-carat teardrop necklace was draped around my neck. A studded-out Cartier watch adorned my wrist, and the fourteen-carat, forty-eight-thousand-dollar princess-cut ring that Carlos picked out sparkled on my finger.

"How long have you two been together?" the jeweler asked as he worked to put everything back in its place. Tempted to tell him a lie, that we had been together for several years, I opted to instead tell the truth.

"It's only been two days since we met," I said proudly.

"Nice," he said with a smile on his face. "Must be something in the air, because you're like the third couple I've come across that have come in and said that they met less than a month ago. Guess that love-at-first-sight thing is real, huh?"

"Yeah," Carlos and I said at the same time.

"Well, that beautiful piece you're wearing on your finger certainly says so."

"That's just a promise ring," Carlos told him. "The real thing will be bigger and better."

He paid for my things, and we said our good-byes as we made our way back outside.

"I'm pretty hungry," I told him. Didn't really want to stop shopping to eat, but I hadn't had anything except for the cold breakfast earlier in the day, and I was beginning to get weak.

"Me too," he said as he handed the valet his ticket stub. We stood hand in hand, playfully kissing on one another, as we waited for our car to come.

"Thank you," I said, surprising myself. Never would've thought that sincere, sweet things would come out of my mouth, but for the last couple of days, I actually meant what I said.

"You deserve it," was all he said back as the

car pulled up. After we got in, he fastened his seat belt and asked, "Where do you want to eat at?"

Instead of driving around aimlessly on an empty stomach, I decided to ask the young valet guy for some suggestions. I cracked the window and got his attention. "We need some place to eat. An expensive place," I said, letting him know what kind of taste I had.

"You will like Lai Wah Heen. It's the celebrity and millionaire hot spot in Toronto, and that's because they're the only ones that can afford it."

After he gave us the directions, we drove off and enjoyed the scenery as we tried to stay on the route the valet gave us.

"We've spent two days together," he reminded. "I've *never* done this before with *any* woman. It makes me feel kind of crazy, but it seems like we're supposed to be together."

I smiled.

Took all his words in.

"Do you have any children?" I asked, not wanting to put off the question any further. "A wife, girlfriend, bitch on the side?"

"Nothing. No kids, wife, girl, nothing. Making money has kept me from all those luxuries. That's why I'm so surprised that I'm with you. This is some shit I wouldn't have even gotten myself into. I'm way too busy for it. What about you?"

"I'm just getting out of a relationship," I

confessed. It was going to be hard to have to make a choice between him and Brooklyn, but if the gypsy was right, the choice was going to have to be made.

"Lucky me," he said as he smiled.

"Yeah, lucky you."

We pulled up to a red light, and he leaned over to kiss me. Took the palm of his hand and tried brushing my hair out of my face, exposing my ear. I jumped. Swatted his hand away.

"What's wrong? Why do you keep doing that?" he asked.

I looked at him and then out my window. My beauty was all I had to get me through in life; it was the only thing I had left of my mother's legacy. And now some of it had faded away. I was still beautiful, but the scars I had made me question my appearance. The ear that had been cut off and replaced with a fake was just too much to bear. Something I didn't want to share with someone else, especially not a man.

"I see your scars," he admitted. "And I don't care what they look like or how you got them. You're beautiful, and I'm happy that I met you. Your heart, your insecurities, and your mind are all safe with me. I promise."

The light turned green, and he drove off. For the first time in my life I felt safe with a man. Totally safe.

"I'm going to get a room at the Westin," he

said as we weaved in and out of traffic. "We'll finish shopping today, relax, and head back to Rochester in the morning."

"No," I blurted out. "Um, I mean, I have to handle something important. Not that this isn't, but . . ."

"Hey, whatever you want," he said calmly. "Whatever you want."

I had to get back to Oshyn, and I refused to be tempted to stay with him any longer. As much as I wanted to, a job needed to be done. I unzipped his pants and dug his big dick out of his boxers. Stroked it with my hands to get it rock hard and bent down to wrap my lips around it.

Sucked it until he squirmed in his seat.

Sucked it until my jaw hurt.

Sucked it until we pulled into the parking lot of the restaurant.

Until he came.

Until all his juice filled my mouth.

Until we were both satisfied.

14

Oshyn

Church to most people was a symbol of love.
Peace.
Happiness.
But church to me was a symbol of death.

Because this was where I came to say my good-byes to too many people who carried pieces of my heart. To too many people who died before their time. To too many people I wished were still here.

I shifted from side to side as I tried to find a comfortable position on the hard wooden pew at Tuff's funeral service. The seats were so worn that if I wasn't careful, a splinter might pierce my skin. I secretly wished there was somewhere else I could be. Wished I had more family that I could go and visit. Wished I didn't feel so alone.

My mind continued to play tricks on me as I wondered what happened to Chloe when she got off the plane. It was as if she'd just disappeared. There was no amount of convincing Brooklyn could do to me that would make me think any differently. I saw her with my own eyes, and I knew for a fact that that was her. By the time we got off the flight, she was gone. Without a trace, which had become her MO.

Forced to be in the second row, Brooklyn and Bella sat next to me as I rocked Mye in my arms. I was afraid that the spirit of death, which I had become accustomed to, would snatch him out of my grasp, so I held my baby close to my breasts, refusing to lose him also.

We were all dressed in black. I had on a basic, tight scoop-neck dress that one would see Jackie O in. Something simple for the occasion. I also wore a small black hat, which I'd pinned to my curls. I allowed the mesh veil that came attached to it to come over my eyes to hide me from the world.

After all this time I couldn't believe that I was back in Rochester, New York. When Chloe kidnapped Mye and pawned him off to Ms. Louise, I swore I'd never return to this city again. There were just too many bad memories here. As it turned out, there were too many bad memories everywhere I went. I had vowed to put the past behind me once and for all, but here I was, at the funeral of a man I had only heard about, the only cousin of my husband.

Trying my best to hide behind my veil, I heard sniffles. Snot being inhaled to the back of a throat. Lots of it. Just the mere sound of sadness made my heart sink, and the hairs on my arms stood up. I looked around at the people who had come to say their last good-byes and saw watery eyes and, for the most part, tears streaming down faces.

Before we got here, I contemplated asking Brooklyn to let me and the kids just stay in our hotel room. We were staying at the Radisson downtown, and I just wanted to rest but decided against asking him. With me acting crazy the last couple of days, I knew that I had lost his trust. My husband felt safer with all of us together. Where he could keep his eyes on us. On me.

The church was packed.

Tuff was not from the Roc, but was bred out of Brooklyn, and also had just got out of prison, which to me slimmed his chances of actually knowing all these people. I found that quite unusual, until I remembered that the people that died in Rochester became stars, if only for a moment, and were just as quickly forgotten.

Weird, I thought to myself as I watched the mourners view the body for the last time. A whiff of death in the disguise of roses breezed past my nose as I inhaled the forest of red flowers that rested alongside his pearl black coffin.

I coughed.

Gagged.

"Oshyn, are you okay?" Brooklyn asked as he quickly started patting my back. I was fine. Just became slightly dizzy and a little nauseous as I recalled having to put that rose on Micah's coffin.

And on Apples's.

And on my grandmother's.

I coughed and gagged again. And again.

"Give me the baby," Brooklyn insisted as he tried prying him from my arms.

"No! No! Get off of him!" I screamed.

In my outside voice again.

I snatched my son back, away from his father's arms, like we were children fighting over a basketball, because I had turned into a mother fighting for her sanity. I watched the crowd turn their attention from the dead body to me. Didn't realize that I was that loud.

"Baby, he can't breathe," Brooklyn said.

Rocking myself back and forth, I looked down and realized that I was holding Mye so tight that his nose was pressing against my chest. My baby *couldn't* breathe. I turned to look at Bella, who still had her earphones glued to her ears, rolling her eyes at me in disgust. Sick of my shenanigans, sick of my bipolar tendencies.

"Let me hold him for just a little bit,"

Brooklyn said, trying not to make more of a scene than I had already caused.

I shook my head no. Just couldn't fathom the idea of my baby not being in my arms. The idea of risking losing him forever. Nobody could protect him like I could, so I needed to make sure that he stayed in the place where he was safest.

My arms.

Brooklyn left the situation alone, and the crowd went back to handling their business. After everyone had their turn, the pallbearers closed the casket. The pastor of the church asked the congregation to rise while he prayed. Everyone obeyed his command except for me. While they stood to their feet, I continued to sit.

Fighting with myself.

Because of the war going on in my mind.

Begging my mind not to flash back to the day when eight pallbearers in dark suits carried two coffins in and out of the church I once loved. The day when the sky cried the tears my eyes could no longer produce. The day Brooklyn stood in the distance and I thought I'd never see him again. Losing the battle, my mind went back to the moment I tried to pick Micah up out of his casket, with the wish to just hug my baby boy one more time.

But his body was stiff.

Cold.

His once soft skin, which had always smelled like baby lotion, now felt like leather and carried the scent of rosemary. His mouth, which had kept me laughing, had been glued together, permanently shutting him up forever.

My baby was not my baby.

His soul was no longer there.

Bella's persistent taps on my shoulder broke me out of my daze, and although we weren't on good terms, and it was incredibly annoying, I was grateful. I was heading downward fast, and she brought me back to reality.

"What?" I whispered to her, wondering how long it had been since everyone took their seats.

"I have to go pee!" she shot back, as usual with a major attitude. She must've been holding it in for a while, because she began squirming in her seat.

"Didn't I tell your little ass to pee before this shit got started?" I waited for a response, which I didn't really want. "You're really working my nerves," I told her through my teeth. "Brooklyn, I'll be right back. I'm going to take Bella to the bathroom really quick."

He looked at me for a moment without saying a word and finally just shook his head from side to side. "No, I'll take her. You just stay here with him," he demanded, pointing to Mye.

"But you have to read the eulogy," I reminded him. "That has to be coming up anytime now."

"It doesn't matter. I'll take her," he insisted as he motioned for her to get up. "And don't you fuckin' move!" he threatened me, just as I had done to Bella seconds before.

They got up and left, heading toward the entrance of the building. My husband had officially turned into my father, which would explain his recent actions. Like why he talked to me the way he did, and why he hadn't touched me in a while.

Since my birthday.

One week ago.

A week of not having sex to most people was normal, but it wasn't for us. Since the day he and I reunited and recommitted our vows to one another, we had made love daily, no matter what. His desire for me was so strong that he wouldn't even let my period deter him from *his* pussy. But lately, since my outbursts, he refused to look at me with the lustful gray eyes I'd become accustomed to. No longer did he spoon me at night, and the sweet nothings he used to whisper in my ears had been replaced with silence. I was no longer the woman he married, but a mere stranger he wished he could get a divorce from.

Missing everything the pastor just said because of my daydreaming, I was at least able to catch him handing the microphone over to a fat lady wearing a purple dress and sporting a big brown Chaka Khan wig. She didn't introduce herself. Never said anything about the deceased. Just belted out a powerful melody of Jesus's healing power.

Those fat people sure know how to sing, I thought to myself, wondering if there was some kind of science that proved that theory. Her voice sent chills up my spine and at the same time startled Mye, as he began to whine. I turned around and looked back to see if I saw any signs of Brooklyn and Bella. I knew I should've taken her myself, I thought as I wondered what was taking them so long. I turned my attention back to the singer, trying to enjoy the rest of the song, while Mye continued to squirm in my arms.

"Shhh, it's okay. Mommy is here," I assured him. My attempt to pacify him was of no help, and suddenly I caught a whiff of the culprit.

A shitty diaper.

I looked behind me again, hoping to see the two of them returning, but all I saw were the mourners. Trying to be a wife that obeyed her husband, I decided to stay put in my seat instead of going to the bathroom and changing him, but Mye's squirms got more and more intense, and his cries grew louder. *I'm going to look back one more time, and if they are not there, I'm just going to go,* I thought, negotiating

with myself. *He'll understand,* I told myse
peeked over my shoulder one more tim

And I saw her.

Again.

My eyes grew wider as I gasped fo
"Chloe's here," I said out loud, by mistak

Even though I could see only the lower
of her face, because of the oversize black
tucky Derby hat that she was using to c
her face, she didn't fool me. I could tell
sister from anywhere.

"Oh!" I screamed, clutching my heart
the hand I had free. "You just scared the
out of me!" I told Brooklyn, wondering
they didn't come back the same way they
He looked at me and rolled his eyes li
bitch.

I wanted to tell him.

Wanted him to see what I saw. There w
way that he could miss it this time. He
know that Chloe was in the same buildir
we were in. I turned around and plant
eyes in the same spot I initially saw her
realized that she was nowhere to be f
imitated Linda Blair's character in *T
cist,* as my head whirled around ur
lably in my attempt to find her.

"What in the hell is wrong with y
Brooklyn yelled, not realizing that
in the church had paused to watch
citement in the second row.

"Like I told you in the bathroom," Bella said, directing her comment to Brooklyn, "she's crazy!"

Too wired up to pimp slap her, I ignored Bella's comments. I had bigger issues to deal with, and this brat was going to have to wait. I turned my attention back to Brooklyn and parted my lips to say something, but nothing came out. My intuition was warning me not to tell him what I saw, but I had to. I grabbed his hand and, with tears streaming down my face, said, "Chloe's here."

"Get the fuck off of me, Oshyn," he said angrily as he snatched his hand out of mine. "Seriously? You're going to do this here? At my cousin's funeral?"

"And now I'd like to call up Brooklyn Jones to read the eulogy," the pastor butted in, sensing that something inappropriate was about to go down.

Without thinking twice, my husband took the first opportunity to get away from me. While he walked into the pulpit, I glanced over my shoulders once more to see if I could get just one more look at her, but there was nothing. Brooklyn stood before the audience, looking handsome as ever, and began his monologue.

"Ummm," he said nervously as he stopped to scratch his head. "He was the only cousin I had. He was funny, charming, and always wanted

to be like me when he grew up," he said in an attempt at humor. It failed. "He—"

He stopped because of what he saw. What I had been trying to get him to see for the longest time. Within a blink of an eye, Chloe had come out of nowhere and was now standing directly in front of the casket, waving at him. He looked at me, and he didn't have to say a word, because his eyes said it all.

He was sorry.

"Is that Chloe?" Bella asked with a trembling voice.

I shook my head yes, right before I dumped Mye into her lap, got out of my seat, and headed to my sister as fast as my black patent leather Louboutin pumps would allow. Chloe turned around and faced me as soon as I reached her.

"Well, hello, Oshyn. It's so good to see you again," she said sarcastically.

I couldn't believe my eyes. I was face-to-face with the woman who killed my whole family. A woman who was supposed to be dead herself, but here she was, in front of me, in front of my husband, alive and well.

I balled up my fist before she was able to get the next sentence out, and punched her dead in the mouth, so hard that she had to catch her fall on the casket. I followed it up with several more body blows that she wasn't able to come back from, and before the people got around to stopping me, I kicked her in the stomach.

Her fumble made the casket rock.

And then I kicked her again.

And again.

And again.

Until she fell on the floor. Sadly, seconds later the casket followed, causing Tuff's body to lie next to hers. Just as I was about to go in on her further, I received a punch in my stomach that knocked me to my knees. I looked around to see where the fist had come from, as I knew Chloe wasn't the culprit. For starters, she was sprawled out on the floor, and the punch I received couldn't have come from a woman. All of a sudden I noticed that Brooklyn had a man pinned up under his body while he beat the shit out of him furiously. One punch after another, he pounded the tall, slender Michael Jordan look-alike.

The guy that I saw sitting next to Chloe.

That bastard must've come to her defense and punched me off of her, I thought, wondering how everything had happened so fast. I was able to get a quick glimpse over at my children, who were still seated where I had left them. Bella and the rest of the audience had their eyes glued on us, not wanting to miss one piece of the action.

While Brooklyn continued to bash the strange dude's head in, I made my way back over to Chloe, who no longer had her hat on, exposing what her evil lifestyle had done to her once beautiful, flawless appearance. Burn marks and scars were now permanent fixtures in her life. While she was getting dudes for money, I remembered trying to warn her that her beauty would fade.

I always knew that she would learn.

The hard way.

By the time I reached Chloe, she had regained some strength and began swinging at me, doing a power punch drill. And just as I was about to swing back, I heard a shot.

One bullet.

A loud one . . . piercing to the ears.

Stopped us in our tracks.

Stopped everyone in their tracks.

I quickly turned to see if the kids were okay, but before my eyes made it to them, I saw Brooklyn fall to his knees in slow motion. Blood spilled out of him as I ran over to him and placed my hands over his, trying my best to keep the blood in, but I couldn't figure out where it was coming from.

"I love you," was the only thing he said as the color began to escape from his pigment.

"No, baby, please don't do this to me. Don't go!" I screamed, but my cries fell on deaf ears as I watched his eyes close and his breaths come to a screeching halt. "No! No! No! No! Come on, baby. Open your eyes. Don't go to sleep. . . . Stay with me!" I felt his soul leave his body as everyone around me reacted frantically.

A female bystander ran to my side and placed her index and middle fingers on his neck. Before I knew it, her once hopeful eyes turned sad. "He's gone," she confirmed.

Chloe and the man that had murdered my husband were nowhere to be found, and I knew that the police were on their way. All of me wanted to stay by his side and just hold him in my arms. I just wanted to be able to tell the police what happened, and be assured that they would handle that bitch once and for all, but I knew that couldn't happen. Couldn't risk them taking me into custody or separating me and the kids.

If I could take his dead and lifeless body with me, I would, but that was impossible. Before I could put too much more thought into it, I got up, drenched in blood, and ran to Bella. Without my having to tell her anything, she grabbed up all of Mye's stuff and ran out of the church with me, and we left the man of our home on the floor, next to his cousin.

May they both rest in peace.

15

Chloe

"I don't have any beef!" Carlos said angrily as he swerved his rental car in and out of traffic, trying to get as far away from the murder scene as he could. "I just shot a man . . . killed him, and it wasn't *my* beef!"

He seemed disturbed by the fact that he had rescued me, but that was something that he would get over. I was floating on cloud nine at the image of him and Brooklyn fighting over me. Over my love. They were the two men that the gypsy had predicted. That bitch did know what she was talking about, I thought as I finally began to feel like I was in heaven again.

"I didn't even want to go to that funeral!" he continued, and he was right. Although we had spent the last two days together, I had to remember that he didn't have to stay with me past all the free pussy I was throwing at him.

But there was something about our union that seemed unbreakable. That seemed real. That seemed predestined.

From the beginning he didn't want to go to the funeral. Rochester wasn't his hometown, and he was in town only to promote another huge event. A Live Nation concert with Jay-Z. A concert that would bring in well over six figures.

He had every right to be mad.

Me and my problems were fucking with his money, but he was a true gentleman for accompanying me, insisting that he didn't want me to go and mourn alone. Especially since I told him who Tuff was to me.

My ex-boyfriend.

With whom I broke up because he started to date my cousin.

I chuckled to myself at the shit I came up with. A lesson I never forgot when it came to dealing with these niggas was that all of them loved a woman that was taken. It heightened my stock. Anything involving another man was better than saying you were single. *Single* screamed desperate, and that was far from what I was.

"What in the hell was that all about, anyway?" he asked, expecting a legit reason for why he had just smoked a dude in broad daylight. One he didn't even know.

"I just wanted to see him one more time before he was buried, but she was there. Oshyn, the one that stole him from me," I lied, trying to drum up some tears from a well that ran dry. "I didn't want to cause a scene, so I went up while everybody was quiet, thinking that she wouldn't say anything in a crowd of mourners, but that bitch has never had any respect for anyone other than herself."

I spoke with my head held down, trying to seem sad about something, trying to disguise the happiness in my voice, which revealed how pleased I was that Brooklyn was out of the picture. Because if I couldn't have him, nobody would.

But Carlos said nothing. There was extreme silence in the car.

Only one of his hands was on the steering wheel, so I grabbed the right one, which lay on his thigh, and whispered, "Thank you."

I was in love.

This was finally my destiny.

Before my dreams of answered prayers could go any further into a future for us, I noticed a black Yukon with blacked-out windows following us. The truck towered over the Benz SL550 that Carlos had rented from the luxury car rental spot. With one monster truck move, we'd be smashed like a can of sardines. Not wanting to involve him in any more avoidable drama, I decided not to mention the stalker.

I wasn't sure when the truck had started

tailing us, but we had been driving for only ten minutes, and I had noticed it following us for at least five of them. We came to a split in the expressway, and Carlos took 390 North, going toward Buffalo, New York, instead of 390 South, which was in the direction of our hotel.

"You don't have to run," I let him know, just in case he was planning his escape route. "This is Rochester. No one snitches, period."

"I'm not worried about that," he assured me, looking in his rearview mirror. "Do you know this truck that is following us?"

I looked behind me, as if I hadn't seen it all along, and shook my head no. The entire truck was pitch black. Even the front windshield was way too dark to see through. *Nah, it can't be,* I thought, trying to shut out the idea that it could be Oshyn. *That bitch doesn't have the balls,* I concluded. But the thought of it actually being her wouldn't go away. My man had just killed her husband, so I was sure that the pair of balls she never had she'd quickly grown.

Suddenly, the truck ran up on us, hitting the back end of our car. *Where are the fucking police when you need them?* I asked myself sarcastically, knowing that I didn't want to see those bastards. I was glad we had our seat belts on, as we jolted forward when the truck hit us again, this time breaking one of the taillights.

"Who in the hell is that?" Carlos asked as he struggled to keep control of the car.

I stayed silent, not really able to come up with any real answers as to who it was or what was going on. Finally tired of playing with us, the driver of the truck hit the gas and pulled along my side of the car, making sure to keep up with our speed.

The window of the truck cracked open. Not far enough to actually reveal her face, just to let us know that there was an actual human in the truck. And then I saw the barrel of a gun slide through the small opening.

"Oh shit, Oshyn found us!" I screamed as I bent down, attempting to get as low to the floor as I could. I knew that the kids were with her, because that bitch wouldn't let them out of her sight, especially with me back in the picture. But I couldn't believe that she would put them in harm's way. She had finally lost her fucking mind. Like I had long ago.

Carlos lost control of the car slightly when he looked over and saw the reason for my sudden panic, and before both of us could react, the trigger was pulled.

The gun fired.

That it was Oshyn had now been confirmed. I could tell by the way she missed the car. No professional would've missed a mark that was so close. That bitch was never gangsta. Just pretended to be.

And then my phone rang. *Probably Tommy,* I thought while ignoring it, but it rang over and over and over again. Something that old man would dare not do. I finally picked it up.

"What!" I asked, agitated. I had just avoided gunshots aimed at me and was in absolutely no mood to play on the phone. The caller hung up, and I knew that it was definitely not Tommy, as the hospital number would have come up on my caller ID, but this number came up private. My phone rang again, and this time I answered it on the first ring.

"Hello?"

No answer.

I put the ringer on silent and threw the phone down on the floor. There were bigger things for me to worry about, like dodging bullets from the woman that wanted me dead the most. We were already going ninety miles per hour on this expressway, but the driver of the Yukon hit the gas and sped past us, jumping in front of our car.

Carlos slammed on his brakes, but he had no choice but to hit the truck, damaging the front end of his rental severely and sending us into a ditch. Oshyn pulled over to the median, stopping a few feet ahead of us.

"Do you have your gun on you?" I asked, after realizing that I had no protection on me.

"No, I got rid of that shit. It was evidence," Carlos remarked.

I quickly began to panic as I watched the

driver's side door swing open, and a pair of legs popped out and touched the ground. With the gun in her hand, and long, luxurious, curly hair flowing from her scalp, I realized that this wasn't Oshyn at all.

"What the fuck?" I said aloud, wondering who this random chick could be. She was absolutely beautiful and thick in all the right places. Like I used to be. And she was definitely my type, sexy and deadly, but I couldn't figure out who her beef was with. I knew Carlos wasn't from here, but he had thrown enough major concerts in this town to learn how to get around as well as he did and to grab a few chicken heads here and there.

"Nina?" he blurted out as she inched closer.

Not sure how he was able to see anything past the barrel of the gun that she had aimed at his head, but men were stupid. All men were stupid.

"Who is she?" I asked as she walked up to his side of the car, but I got no answer. A few cars whisked past us, going way too fast to notice the danger we were in. With no protection to save us, we were on our own.

"Who is she?" the girl asked, pointing the gun at me. "Is she the reason you don't come home anymore?"

"Nina, are you fucking crazy? How did you find me?" Carlos asked, with an obvious hint of confusion in his voice.

"I tapped your phone. Sprint Family Locator. Only five dollars additional each month. Tells me everything. Where you are, where you just came from, how long you stayed, what route you took to get there. Everything."

"So, you drove all the way here from the city? That's five hours," he said, confused.

She stared at him, not really seeming to want to answer the question, but she did, anyway. "I knew I couldn't get you in Saint-Tropez, and you stopped answering my calls, so I came to you." She paused. Then looked at me. "So, this broke, busted bitch is the reason?"

"Fuck you," I blurted out. I knew I was taking a chance talking shit with no weapon, but I couldn't just let her talk to me like that. It would have ruined my reputation.

"What did you say?" she asked as she took the gun off of Carlos and pointed it back in my direction.

"I said fuck—"

The gun went off again.

This bitch is crazy, I said to myself, laughing, as I tried to figure out where the bullet had gone. I definitely wasn't hit.

She couldn't shoot for shit, but she was certifiably crazy. I found her amusing. Not a threat anymore, but more like entertainment. If she wanted to shoot us, she would've done it by now, but by her reckless actions, it was clear she wasn't a true gangsta like me. She played too much. Liked the attention. She was a pussy. Smelled her from a mile away.

"Say one more thing and I'm going to blow your fucking brains out!" she warned.

"Yeah, a'ight," I said sarcastically.

"What?"

"Man, talk to your nigga. I don't have shit to do with your situation," I roared.

Tired of watching us talk back and forth, Carlos took control of the situation by getting out of the car. Guess he sensed her lack of seriousness about actually shooting someone, also, as he no longer seemed afraid to take action.

"Where is my son at?" he asked her.

"Son? You don't have a son anymore, bastard! Make one with this bitch. My son is with his new fath—"

Before the last part of her words could be formed, Carlo took Nina's long locks, entangled them tightly in his fingers, and smashed her head into the hood of the wrecked Benz. When he lifted her head back up, it was filled with blood, and before I got a chance to see what other damage had been done, he took her head and rammed it through the glass windshield, cracking it. She lifted her head with her mouth open, and I noticed that this time teeth were missing.

"Don't you ever talk like that about my son again, you stupid bitch!" he warned. After knocking her teeth out, he threw her on the ground and stomped her out. She lay motionless as his thrusts got more aggressive. When he finally came to a stop, he ordered me out of the car.

"For what?" I asked him, confused. "You're not going to beat the shit out of me!"

"Man, get out! We can't drive in this car anymore. We're going to get in the truck."

So much for this rental, I thought as I noticed all the irreparable damage that had been done. I opened the door and got out, then made my way to the other car. "What about the rental? Can this be traced back to you?"

"Come on, baby, don't let my image fool you. I'm a street dude. Nothing can be traced back to me." We both got in the truck and drove away. Together at last.

Me, Bonnie.

Him, Clyde.

16

Oshyn

I lay curled up in a fetal position in the corner of my hotel room. Mye cried hysterically, while Bella did all she could to calm him down, but to no avail. He wanted his mother's love and his father's touch, but neither was at his disposal. Brooklyn's touch had been torn from our grasp forever, while my heart had been ripped to shreds.

Irreparable.

Like shattered glass.

At least an hour had floated by since we rushed out of the funeral, leaving Brooklyn all alone at his own murder scene. The place where he went to bid farewell to someone else's life was the same place where his very own life came to a cruel end. I continued to rock my pain away as Mye reached for me.

Unable to be the mother he needed me to be, Bella took control by picking him up off the bed. She walked him around the room, trying as best as she could to soothe him, something I knew she needed herself.

Because we were all hurting.

My baby's cries grew quieter and quieter as I smothered my tears in the last T-shirt my husband had on before we left earlier that day. I inhaled his sweet, sweaty scent and instantly began to cry.

"My last words to him weren't I love you!" I screamed, startling Mye again into the same sea of tears that had taken Bella so long to stop.

Normally, she would've said something smart by now, but death had taken its toll on her as well. By the way she looked at me, she knew that I needed her help, so she walked over to me with my baby in her hands and sat down beside me.

She didn't say anything. Just sat there speechless while I lost my mind. She even attempted to stroke my hair, which had become out of control, but nothing helped. I was now a widow to the man I was supposed to grow old with. To the man who stole my heart the very first time I laid my eyes on him. To the man who asked me to be his wife.

I remembered the first time I saw him at church, two years ago, in North Carolina. I couldn't keep my eyes off of him, and then we officially met at the bookstore later that day. I recalled giving him such a hard time when he tried to pay for my books, but all he was trying to be was a gentleman. Just didn't want to admit to myself that I could actually love again, especially after all the drama I had gone through with Micah's dad, Trent.

My mind went back to the night I placed my hand in his and stared into his light gray eyes, saying yes when asked to be his wife. It was like destiny refused for me and Brooklyn to be apart. Even the heartache of catching him in the bed with Chloe while we were on our honeymoon wasn't strong enough to separate us. Because he was my Adam and I was his Eve. Our souls had been melded together, and the little piece of life I had left had died with him.

I had become the living dead.

Then, out of nowhere, Bella snapped me out of my dreams with her cries. Millions of tears stormed out of her eyes as she showed how physically upset she was. And then she spit it out. Big brown chunks of what she had to eat for the day now laid next to us as we did the best we could to handle the situation. Couldn't believe that we weren't used to this by now, because we weren't amateurs at mourning death. As her crying outburst simmered down, I heard a knock at the door.

"Be quiet," I whispered to her in an attempt to calm her whimpering down. "Shhhh, somebody is knocking on the door."

She wiped a few tears away from her face and stared at the same door that my eyes had become glued to.

"I didn't hear anything," she said, confused. I caught her looking at me from my side view as she continued. "Did you hear me? I don't think anyone is at the—"

"Shhhh," I repeated. "I heard it again." I stood to my feet, not knowing what my next move would be. "Maybe it's Brooklyn," I said, with a hint of excitement in my voice. I managed to crack a grin just at the thought of seeing the small gap that accompanied his smile.

Not being able to bear the thought of it being my husband on the other side of the door, I ran to it and unlatched the locks that kept us away from each other. I opened the door with expectancy in my heart, not able to contain the feeling of him in my arms one more time.

"Brooklyn?" I said as I turned my head from side to side, staring down the hotel hallway. "Brooklyn, where are you?"

"It's not him," I heard a woman's voice say, and then I saw her. She was just as beautiful as the last time I laid my eyes on her.

"Mama?"

"Jes, it's jur grandmother, and I come to help ju."

I let her in and closed the door behind us, noticing that her Puerto Rican accent was as strong as before.

"Oh my goodness," she continued as she placed her old, wrinkly hands over her mouth. "Jus look at Bella. She is so big and *muy bonita*. And the baby *es muy grande*. Oh, I just wish Micah could see this!"

"I missed you so much, Mama. How are Micah and Apples doing?"

"Oh, don't ju worry about them. They are both doing fine," she assured me.

I wanted to bombard her with questions regarding them, but she didn't seem like she came to talk about it.

"Auntie, what's going on?" Bella asked, with a terrified look on her face. "Who are you talking to?"

"Don't you see her? It's Mama . . . my grandmother. Don't you remember her?" I asked as I pointed in her direction.

"But . . . but . . . nobody is there," Bella responded slowly. Her body seemed to tense up, and her voice trembled as she continued. "Why are you talking to yourself?"

"Don't be rude!" I shot back at her. "You *will* respect her!" I turned back to my grandmother, who had taken a seat on the bed, and apologized for Bella's smart mouth. "I just don't know what has gotten into her lately," I confessed as I sat down beside her.

"It's okay, baby. Ju are jus stressed from what

happened today. But I came to tell ju that everything is going to be jus fine." And before she got another word out, I broke down.

"She was supposed to be dead, but she managed to take him from me!"

"You're scaring me," Bella said, interrupting me. "What's going on?"

"Don't you see me speaking to a grown-up?"

"Shhh. Calm down, sweetheart. She's jus scared, too, ju know? Been through a lot herself, but don't get angry with her. Be patient, and she'll grow up to be a good woman." I missed her wisdom and her meek spirit dearly as she calmed me down instantly. "Ju know what ju have to do?"

"What?" I asked, thinking that she was still referring to Bella.

"Ju have to get rid of her once and for all. Kill Chloe. That's the only way."

Kill Chloe, I thought to myself as I wondered what would make her say that to me. That was out of her character. Something that she would have never recommended to me on any other day, but maybe there was something she knew that I didn't.

"That child is evil and must be put down, but ju are the only one that can do it. If ju don't, she will murder ju and the rest of jur children. A slow and painful death. This is jur warning."

"But how am I going to do that? I can't take

them with me. That'll be leaving them in too much danger, and I don't have anyone I can trust them with."

"Ju go and I will watch over them. Everything will be okay, I promise."

I looked at Bella, who was sobbing silently in the corner, and then took a quick glance at Mye, who was sound asleep in her arms. I walked over to her and kneeled down to talk to her.

"I have to go now," I told her. "I have to take care of Chloe before she comes back to hurt you guys."

"No, please don't leave us here," Bella pleaded with me, visibly scared out of her mind.

"No, everything is going to be okay," I promised as I kissed her forehead. "I need you to be strong now. Take care of Mye for me, and I'll be back to get the both of you tomorrow."

"But I can't take care of a baby. . . . I'm only nine," she revealed, as if I didn't know.

"You'll do fine. Just order room service for your food, and fix Mye those bottles," I said, pointing to the refrigerator. "I'll be back before you run out. And my grandmother will be here, too. Don't worry. You won't be alone."

"Please don't leave me here with a ghost. You were talking to a dead person! Please don't go. . . . I'm so scared." Snot now fell as freely out of her nose as the tears from her eyes.

"Oshyn, it's time. Ju have to go now," Mama said, hinting that I should say my good-byes.

I kissed Bella again and planted my lips on my son, praying that I would see them both again. But this was something I knew I had to do if we were going to live a long life. I walked toward the door, and when I reached it, I grabbed onto the handle, looking back one more time at my family.

"Kill her," was the last thing I heard as I walked out, not having a clue what I was getting ready to get myself into.

17

Oshyn

Nine thirty in the morning.

The iHop parking lot.

It was where I had slept.

It was a brand-new day, and I still found myself on the hunt for Chloe. The four hours of sleep had done some good, but my mental state still needed work. The violent tosses and turns I endured while trying to get some rest had pretty much kept me up the entire night. The nightmare that I wished was just a dream had come true, and now haunted me in my attempts to get some sleep. No matter how hard I tried, I couldn't get Brooklyn out of my mind. Couldn't get the fact that he had died in my arms out of my mind. I couldn't get anything out of my mind.

Even though I was in the hood, I didn't

worry about anyone coming to attack me. My life had already been ruined, so if somebody came at me . . . they would be the one in shock. My knife fit snugly in my front pocket and was easily accessible. I wasn't the Oshyn everyone thought they knew. I was the new Oshyn. The Oshyn who'd lost her husband. The Oshyn who was now all alone. And the Oshyn who would learn to commit murder.

The sound of the word *murder* caused my neck to swivel toward the passenger seat. I had to make sure my two-toned tan sack was still on the floor. Its contents—duct tape, rope, Mace, and acid—were all important to me. Crucial to the mission. I leaned forward, spotted the sack, then started up the vehicle.

As soon as I adjusted my mirror, I got a wake-up call. My hair was matted and spread all over my head. With my bare hands I patted my head, hoping to do enough to get by. It was bad enough not having a change of clothes or a washcloth to clean my face, but my hair needed to lie down to keep me from looking crazy. Couldn't risk any unwanted attention being drawn to me. I needed to get rid of her and get out of this city as fast I could.

When I pulled out of the lot, I realized the gas tank was close to empty, so gas was at the top of my list. What else could be expected? I had spent all night looking for Chloe and had driven around for hours with no luck. I had even checked where we used to live.

Nothing.

Not one sign of that bitch.

I wasn't sure why, but I'd even checked my grandmother's old neighborhood. It was her suggestion. She'd coached me, even told me a new way to get there. Her neighbor, Miss Rose, was surprised to see me, but after she told me why, I understood. Chloe had indeed been through the neighborhood and had told Miss Rose that I was dead. No longer on the face of the earth. I told her that if she saw Chloe again to call me. I then went on a rampage to find her, since I knew she was still in town.

Chloe had no friends that I could turn to for answers. She could never keep even one, not even an associate. Always fucked their men behind their backs, or simply stabbed them in the back. I was in this alone and wasn't looking forward to the mission. It was almost 10:00 a.m., and no new clues, and I had become incredibly frustrated. A hint of emotion took over.

Within seconds, I pulled over, put the car in park, and burst into tears. In that quick instance, images of my husband flooded my mind. I cried out like a baby, wishing he were with me. I thought about his sweet touch, his soft lips, and the way he took care of me.

"Why, Brooklyn! Whyyy!" I bawled. I banged my head against the wheel and sobbed some more. "I need you, baby. I need you! Do you hear me, Brooklyn?"

I had become enslaved to my emotions, which was why it took more than an hour for me to bounce back. I had to keep sniveling and sniffling up my snot, trying to get myself together. To be able to drive within the white lines again. Then my big break came. The phone rang, and the call was from a Rochester area code. It didn't take long for me to answer and get the 411 on Chloe. My investigative work had paid off. I told an old classmate, "You saw her where? You sure it was Chloe?"

I questioned hard.

I hung up in a rage and started down highway 490 East, then got off at Clinton Avenue, just three exits down. It was a trashy neighborhood, dirty. A place I wasn't feeling at all. A far cry from Saint-Tropez, it was where crackheads roamed and all the welfare recipients hung out. As I drove down Clinton, I noticed the going-out-of-business signs that hung high in some windows, and the boarded-up spots where the owners had just given up.

I stopped dead in my tracks when I spotted her. She was outside an old factory that had closed down near Hart Street. My mind raced, wondering what she was up to and how I would make my move. It looked as if she'd just had a meeting with someone in an old Buick. I just wasn't 100 percent sure.

Before she could make it back to her car, I revved the gas and picked up speed. I found myself chasing her onto the sidewalk, and she began to run like a bat out of hell. It was like something out of the movie *Heat*. No holds barred. It amazed me how fast her ass could run, six-inch spiked heels and all. She'd never done anything athletic as a child. Guess her life being on the line brought changes.

Quick changes.

I was sure I looked crazy the way I gripped the wheel with both hands and leaned as far into it as I could go. But fortunately the lot was mostly bare, with the exception of a few bystanders, who either held brown paper bags containing liquor or were looking for their next hit.

I heard someone yell out, "Look at her!" They pointed at me, then attempted to point at Chloe, until she made it to the end of the deserted strip mall and darted around the back.

Like a madwoman, I followed her and swerved the car off the sidewalk onto the pavement and turned on two wheels toward the back. Wherever Chloe had gone, I was sure she was out of breath. It didn't matter where she had run off and hid, or what kind of gun she had, because I wasn't going to back down. Not this time. I kept my grip tight, while rotating my neck from side to side, trying to sniff out any kind of movement. That was when I saw it. The long denim part of her shirt.

She moved like a snake behind a big blue trash can nestled behind the factory warehouse door. I revved the gas again, picked up speed, and in no time stopped abruptly in front of the closing door. I was sure she thought she had escaped. That just simply wasn't the case.

I had her.

I knew it.

For the first time, my own blood will die at my hands, I told myself, hopping from the car. I almost forgot my sack, but I doubled back, grabbed it, and made the alarm on the door chirp. I didn't care if Chloe knew I was coming in. Because I wanted her to know that her time here on earth was coming to an end.

Inside, things felt eerie. There was a damp feeling, and the smell of mildew accompanied it. I took baby steps while searching for a light switch, all along watching my back. The darkness had me spooked, plus the fact that Chloe was a slick bitch. I kept doing police moves, stopping at every corner before I moved farther.

Then I saw her.

Standing three yards away from me.

We faced each other like two boxers headed to our corners of the ring. It was weird, because all sort of emotions flooded my body. To me, she was beautiful. She was family. But today I would keep our family tradition alive. She would die at the hands of me and would be buried before her time. But truth be told, she was my cousin, my sister, one of my few remaining living relatives.

"Oshyn. My dear Oshyn," Chloe called out to me. Her heels clicked on the hard floor, and she grinned wickedly. "So good to see you," she said, with disdain in her voice. "This is good." She nodded and paced the floor like it was a good thing we were now in the same room.

I walked toward her, making sure I kept my confidence up. I had thrown my sack over my shoulder, and I kept my right hand near the front pocket of my jeans. I couldn't help but wonder if she, too, had a weapon. Oddly enough, she kept her fingers at her sides.

"We need to talk, Chloe. I mean, we're family." I made a funny movement with my cheeks, then purred like a harmless kitten.

She snarled. "Most of your family is dead, bitch. They just waiting on you." She laughed wildly.

Out of the blue, I dug into my pocket, flipped open my blade, and let a victory grin seep through the sides of my lips. As I held the knife in her direction, her facial expression changed.

"Look here, cuz, sis, or whatever you want to call me. Let me put your dumb ass onto something. I think you really need to know some good news since Brooklyn's dead."

Damn, it was about my late husband. And it was good? Maybe I did need to know, I told myself, getting choked up again.

"Why, Chloe? Why did it happen?"

She moved closer, and so did I. For once, she was sincere as she told me the guy she was with at the funeral had tried to kill her, too. He was trying to frame her. When she told me that he followed her to the funeral and made his move on her there, I was shocked. I felt bad for her, just as I thought about my honey once again. Chloe could see the sadness in my face as I wept like a baby in front of her. The tough girl role had come to an end momentarily.

I threw my hands across the upper part of my face in an attempt to hide my misery. The blade stuck out from my fingers, but I still had a decent grip. Huge tears began to blur my vision. But they didn't bother my sense of touch. It was Chloe behind me. I could feel her coldness and her senseless touch. Without warning, she managed to snatch the weapon from my hand and wrap her dominant arm around my neck. Slowly she told me I was still naive. Still stupid. And now I would be joining Grandma, Apples, Micah, and Brooklyn in the depths of hell.

Chloe had tricked me.

I should have known better.

And now I would pay for my stupidity.

She inched me along, still with a good grip on my neck, looking for a place to settle. Finally, she led me to the only chair in the place. From what I could see, it was metal, uneven, and had barely enough space to hold my plump ass. It didn't matter. Chloe had the blade pressed deep into the skin of my neck and refused to allow me the freedom to move even an inch. My bottom was placed as she sat me, until she snatched the rope from my sack and began to tie me up with her left hand, while still letting the knife hold my neck hostage with her right hand. At first the rope seemed to be loose, until she had me in a controlling bundle. Then it became tighter and tighter as she looped the rope around several more times.

I flinched a little as the rope tightened, yet my soul wouldn't allow me to show any fear. That was what she had been used to all our lives. She assumed that I was scared of anything that didn't look or smell right. And she, the rebel, the gangsta bitch, reacted with malice in every situation that came her way. Next, she probed my feet. She grinned, then went for the duct tape. It was crazy how she was now using all my tactics against me. Why was I the one sitting in the chair?

My little pep talk about showing no fear

meant nothing anymore. The moment I saw Chloe pick up a long iron piece that had been left on the cold concrete floor, my heart began thumping at a rapid pace, and tears welled up in my eyes. Everything was happening so fast. Too fast, my body warned. But there was nothing more I could do. Chloe beat the rod-shaped weapon against her forearm as she moved my way. Her eyes revealed that she would go all the way. Her smirk told me this was a long time coming.

"C'mon, Chloeee! Nooo! Let's talk about—"

Before I knew it, she'd hit me over the head.

Hard.

Again.

And again.

Until I no longer responded.

18

Oshyn

"Remember Trent?" Chloe asked me casually, as if we were two girlfriends out for Sunday brunch. As if we were the reminiscing type. As if he wasn't the father of my firstborn son.

I sat on the steel chair as I slowly regained consciousness, with my hands tied tightly together. The same had been done to my feet, giving me no chance to escape. The blood that had trickled down from my head now replaced the saliva that was in my mouth. I wasn't quite sure what the damage looked like, but the amount of blood that fell and the intense throbbing pain I felt let me know that it was serious. Even though I had started to see double, I refused to give up, but at the present moment, my odds of killing Chloe were looking very slim.

"Did you hear me?" Chloe asked me.

I couldn't figure out what she was hinting at by mentioning Trent, so I never answered her question. Just sat restlessly in pain as I tried to calculate what her next move was going to be, so I could be prepared for what was to come next.

She balled up her fist and hit me with two powerful back-to-back punches in the face, leaving me in excruciating pain, but I never cried. Never even made a sound. Couldn't give her the satisfaction of knowing that she had hurt me more than she thought she had.

I just refused to let her take that away from me.

Like she had done everything else in my life.

"Damn it, answer me when I'm fucking talking to you!" she demanded, until she was satisfied that she had gotten my attention. "Now, I'll ask you again. . . . Do you remember Trent?"

I nodded my head yes, trying my best to defy her orders. But the next punch she threw landed on my jaw and instantly sent chills down my spine. The blood now poured down my face like a bloody sea, and it was then that I realized that if I had any hope of surviving, I was going to have to play by her rules.

"I have all day," she admitted as she rubbed

the hand that assaulted me. "I've dreamed about this day ever since you left me for dead at that old warehouse, and the day is finally here! And now you're in a warehouse. Seems appropriate, doesn't it?"

I heard the excitement that rose in her voice as she spoke about the torture she had planned for me all this time. The excitement from the thought of my demise. The excitement from the thought of her being responsible for it. Before she got a chance to finish her speech, I broke my silence.

"Yes, I remember Trent. I remember him."

She smiled.

Pleased that I made the choice to give in.

Pleased that she was breaking me down.

Pleased that this was going to be easier than she thought.

"I don't know if our grandmother told you, but I fucked him, too. She caught us in her bed . . . you know, after he put you out. While you were pregnant and in the middle of that snowstorm. Since this is the end of your life, I thought you'd like to be aware of that."

I went back to the day when the man who introduced me to love threw me out of our home and watched through the bedroom window we once shared as I went into labor, with the bank of snow as my bed. Chloe admitting that she had sex with him wasn't a surprise to me, because I expected nothing better from either of them, so she could've kept her confession to herself. Realizing that her bringing up Trent didn't matter to me, she continued to dig further to gain some kind of reaction from me.

"You stupid bitch, you were never able to keep a man," Chloe revealed, with a smirk on her face. "I fucked them all, but Brooklyn was the best."

She had struck a nerve, and my blood instantly began to boil.

"He never loved you!" I blurted out, letting her know that despite how I acted, her words were slowly breaking me down.

At that moment, she laughed a laugh that was so loud that it bounced off the walls. She was cracking herself up at my inability to control myself.

My emotions.

"Oh, trust and believe that he loved me," she said after catching her breath. "I was having his baby, and it was a pregnancy that was planned. And you killed it. You killed our future, our destiny, our love, and I've returned the favor by killing him. Dead. Like you'll be not too long from now."

And out of nowhere, I started laughing. So hard that it bounced off the same walls Chloe's laughter once did.

"What in the fuck is so funny?" she asked, confused.

"You are."

Before I went any further, I spit out some

blood that had taken over my mouth, and contemplated choosing my words wisely, but then decided against it, as my fate at this point seemed inevitable.

"You always had my sloppy seconds. You may have fucked all my boyfriends, but you had them after me. Step up your game, boo. I know it may be a little harder now that I fucked your face up like that, but maybe after I'm gone and out of the way, you can get a nigga on your own. I won't be a threat anymore, so you don't have to worry about him falling in love with me first."

If I didn't know any better, I could've sworn that I saw steam coming out of her nose. I had her hot.

"I have a man," she revealed, in an artless attempt to upstage me in the arena of love.

"Yeah, I'm sure you do." I rolled my eyes, which was followed by an instant throbbing of my face where she'd struck it.

But I didn't flinch.

Didn't want her to know that she hurt me, because I knew that there was more to come.

"My man is more successful than Brooklyn ever was. Carlos has more money, a bigger dick, and more balls. As a matter of fact, he proved it by killing your husband . . . for me."

I noticed a twinkle in her eye as she continued to speak highly of the man who took Brooklyn's life.

"I hope that your children come out retarded and you die giving birth to those bastards," was all I could think of to say.

She walked over to a small black table and picked up a book of matches. She then lit one and sat the tip of the burning flame on the corner of my eye.

"Owww! Owww!" were the words that replaced the smart comments as I felt my skin melting off. She threw the old match on the floor and took another one out, swiping it against the matchbook.

"No . . . no . . . no!" was all I could muster up as she sat the flame on my lip. All I heard was a sizzling sound, and it felt like my skin was being fried.

"How does it feel to be burned?" she asked, pointing to the scars on her face from the third-degree burns she'd sustained.

I didn't answer. Knew it was a trick question. Knew that there was no right or wrong answer. I knew that anything I said would lead to my doom.

Noticing that my cooperation was out of the question, she walked back over to the table and picked up a jar that looked to contain two cockroaches. She slowly unscrewed the top as the roaches ran around at lightning speed at just the thought of being free once again. She picked one up and brought it over to me, holding it close to my face.

Its long antennae and legs wiggled around as its big brown body followed suit, trying to get its captor to let go, but Chloe held on tighter. I tried my best to move my face out of the way as she inched it closer and closer.

"What are you doing?" I asked, struggling to get my hands free.

She remained silent as she aimed the roach at my ear. I violently yanked my head back and forth, trying my best to get her away from my ear, but nothing seemed to work.

Tired of my fighting, Chloe put me in a headlock and stuffed the roach in my ear, and all of the fighting I did proved to be useless, as the roach seemed to make its way into my ear canal.

"Ahhhhh!" I screamed as the crippling pain of the insect burrowing too far in my ear became unbearable. *Excruciating torture* were the only words I could use to describe the feeling I had as I listened to the roach make a home inside my head.

"Get it out of me!" I yelled, while the movement of its crunchy body echoed in my ear.

"Guess what I found out about roaches?" she asked, as if we were in a class. "I learned that they can go, like, a week or two without water. Those bastards can even go for several hours without air."

Satisfied that the first roach was lodged deep enough in my ear, she went back to the jar to retrieve the second one from the glass prison it had somehow found its way back into. I began to bang my head as hard as I could against my shoulder as I felt the disgusting creature tunneling into my brain.

"When I get out of here, I'm going to kill you, bitch!" was all I could say as she inserted the other roach into the ear that was free. She stayed put for a little bit, making sure that it had dug itself deep into my canal, and then she walked away.

Although I wondered where she went, I was more concerned with relieving myself of this pain. Then she appeared again out of nowhere with a bucket full of water.

"I'm done playing with you. Let's just get this over with. Tell me where the kids are."

Even with all the racket going on in my brain, I heard every word she said, but chose to ignore her as my head did the dance of one who was possessed. Letting me know that she meant business, Chloe took my head and slammed it into the bucket of water and held it down while I tried my hardest to get up. It was probably a few seconds, but it felt like eternity before she let my head back up for some air.

I gasped for as much air as my lungs would allow, but with the roaches still running rampant in my mind, I began to panic, losing all the extra air that I had left.

"Where are Bella and Mye?" she asked again, with a dead serious face that warned me against trying her.

She was officially done playing with me and

was getting ready to prove it. Even though I wasn't ready to die, I still wasn't able to give my children up for the sake of my freedom.

"Go and kill yourself," was the last thing I said before she plunged my head back into the water.

My hair floated around carelessly as I held my breath, trying to get a hold of whatever air I could. And then I panicked again, after realizing that I was no longer being afforded the luxury of air. I began to rapidly move my body in an attempt to free myself, but my movements only got me more excited. I fought it for as long as I could, as my breathing reflexes slowly came back.

And I inhaled.

While my head was still submerged under water.

Before I took another breath, Chloe pulled my head out as I coughed and gagged violently. Trying my best to survive. And then her phone rang.

"Damn it," she said to herself after taking the phone out of her pocket and reading the name on her caller ID. "I forgot that I was supposed to meet up with Carlos for dinner later on." After talking to herself, she finally decided to answer the phone. "Hey, baby. Sorry I . . ."

She paused.

Then she said, "Who is this . . . ? Nina?" I watched her reaction closely as she paused again, assuming to let whoever this Nina chick was talk. "Can I meet you? Ummm, yeah. When? Now? Okay, give me a few minutes and I'll meet you at the Marketplace Mall."

Chloe asked me once more where the children were, and after I refused to tell her, she dumped my head back in the bucket and kept it in there until this time I lost consciousness.

19

Chloe

I pulled into the parking lot of the Market-place Mall about twenty minutes after I hung up the phone with Nina. It had only been a couple of days since I watched my man put her head through the windshield of his rental car, and I was curious to see what she looked like. I was still very confused about what she was doing with Carlos's phone, and my mind was running a million miles per second, trying to drum up the answers. But I was finally here, and I was sure that she would tell me everything I needed to know.

It was her idea to meet here at the mall, which let me know that this wasn't her first trip to Rochester. I walked into the mall, took a seat at one of the tables in the food court, and glanced at my watch.

"This bitch needs to hurry up!" I said out loud, wondering what was taking her so long. I had to get back to Oshyn so that I could get rid of her once and for all.

I looked around and realized that nothing ever changed in this city, and certainly not in the old-ass mall. It had been over two years since I had actually stepped foot in this place, and everything still looked exactly the same. The stores looked the same, and all the people still looked the same. I remembered the trips to the mall that my mother would take me on as a little girl and how excited I was to just be with her.

And now resentment had taken its place, because my childhood memories of her were slowly fading away, and this was one of the only places I could recall spending time with her. However, before my mind wandered any further into the excruciating pain of missing her, I noticed Nina sitting at a table not too far from mine.

Watching me.

Closely.

Damn, I'm falling off, I thought to myself as I wondered why I never saw her. And so I stared back at her, not really knowing what game we were playing, but not wanting to let her win, either. *This is a weird-ass bitch!*

Although I wanted to play this petty-ass, childish game with her, I realized that time wasn't on my side, because I still had things to settle with Oshyn. So I decided to get up to see what this meeting was all about. I walked over to her table and sat down across from her as she took a sip from her Starbucks cup.

"Who are you?" she asked as she pushed her oversize Emilio Pucci shades up on her nose. I assumed the glasses were hiding her eyes, which, I would bet, were black. She had a few bruises and small cuts from the windshield glass on her face, and I noticed that the front teeth that had fallen out were now back in place. Despite all the bang ups her body had endured, she was still sexy.

"So, you got your teeth back?" I asked, ignoring her dumb-ass question. I wanted her to know that I was in control of this and that she would follow my lead.

"They were fake, anyway," she said nonchalantly as she waved her hand with an "I don't care" motion. "Carlos knocked my real ones out years ago, when I was twenty-four, so now when he punches me in the mouth, I can normally just pop them right back in."

Damn, I thought, not believing that she was being so candid with me. *I have to watch her. She has something up her sleeve.*

And she continued. "But you never answered my question. Who the fuck are you?" She took another sip of whatever was in her cup and brushed back a few flyaway hairs that

had popped out of her extremely long ponytail with her fingers.

And then waited.

For an answer.

"Who the fuck are *you?*" was my response.
She didn't hesitate to give an answer.

"I'm Carlos's wife. The mother of his only
son. The woman he chose to spend the rest of
his life with until death do us part. That's who
the fuck I am. Now, like I said, who the fuck
are you, and what are you doing with my husband?"

She grabbed her Louis Vuitton Damier bag
and unzipped it, taking out a pack of Newport
cigarettes. Shorts. She stuck one in her mouth
and then waited again.

For an answer.

I couldn't help but crack a smile at her. Because she was a comic who didn't realize how
funny she actually was. But she was a sloppy
comic who hadn't done her homework, because if she had, she would know who I was
and why I was no one to fuck with. This was no
secret. It was a known fact that everyone in my
city had become accustomed to, and those
muthafuckas stayed out of my way.

"Don't make me have to ask you again,"
Nina said as she lit her cancer stick up, taking
a pull and blowing it in my face. "Who . . .
are . . . you?"

"I'm the bitch that will kill you while your

son watches, and then will stab him to death after you stop breathing. I'm the bitch that will set you on fire and watch you dance around until you burn to death. I'm the bitch that will bury you alive and watch in pure pleasure while the last breaths you inhale are dirt. I'm the last of the Mohicans. A true definition of the word *gangsta*. I'm a killer. A murderer. I do this for fun because I can and nobody will stop me. I fuck who I want, when I want, and right now it's your *nigga*."

Had to catch my breath before I continued.

"So, before we go any further with this—whatever the fuck this is—watch what you say to me." I paused for a few seconds to let that set in. "I don't know if you chose this spot because it is in public, but be warned that I don't give a fuck where we are. Unlike you, I don't shoot and miss." I put a smile back on my face, extended my hand, and said, "It's a pleasure to meet you."

Expecting her to say something else smart, I was very surprised when she extended her hand and shook mine. It was something I definitely didn't expect after the monologue of threats I had just issued.

"So, what's up?" I asked, trying to get to the point of this crap after the awkward ice-breaker we had just shared.

"I simply want to know what the deal is with you and my husband. That bastard won't give me any answers, so I figured we could talk woman to woman to get this shit straight and clear up some of the confusion. How long have you known him?"

"Well, babe, I'm not a woman-to-woman type of bitch, but I've known him for about a week, and it was love at first sight."

She erupted into laughter. Laughed so hard that she inhaled the nicotine down the wrong pipe and began to choke.

"Oh my goodness, now that was some hilarious random shit to say." She stopped to cough a few more times, cleared her throat, then continued. "One week? You've known *my* husband for one week, and now you're in love? That's that dumb shit they must do up here in Rochester. You ain't no real New York bitch!"

"Nah, boo, this is that dumb shit we do here in Rochester."

I grabbed an old, used plastic knife that hadn't been thrown away by the last person and, without thinking twice, slid my hand under the table and rammed it into her thigh. Her cries of pain startled the few people that were actually eating, and I warned her to shut up.

"I'm a Roc bitch for life, and don't you ever forget it," I stated.

She continued to moan in agony as I took the bloody knife out of her skin and placed it back on the table. Small evidence of what I was capable of, and what I would do again if she said some more slick shit.

But she didn't budge.

Didn't get up and storm out, like I had assumed she would, but then again, deep down inside I knew she was going to stay. Any woman that had her teeth knocked out *often* wouldn't let a simple plastic knife wound stop her. She was a woman with a purpose, and she wasn't going to leave until she got what she came here for.

Her husband.

"I'm sorry," she confessed. For the first time since I sat down, I was calm enough to hear her thick New York City accent. It amazed me that, although we were from the same state, we sounded nothing alike. There was no common ground between the city and upstate New York, and personally, I was glad.

Upstate niggas got slept on.

The NYC boys came up here and got put to sleep for life.

"I know you don't have anything at all to do with this, but I just had my son. He's not even a month old, and this nigga is out here fucking you. He left me for you," she said confused, with a hint of disgust in her voice. And then she continued. "I mean, after all I've done for him. I bailed his sorry ass out of jail, and that shit was so high, it took me and three of my aunts to put houses up to get him released. And he still ain't paid them back yet. He was broke not too long ago, and I'm the one who put his ass back on, and now he wants to leave me?"

"Look, I don't argue well, so what is the point of this? What are you trying to say? From what you're saying, Carlos seems like he doesn't want to fuck with you or your son anymore, so you probably just need to move on with your life."

"No," she said defiantly as she shook her head from side to side. "My family will be back together. If that's the last thing I do, we will be happy again, and he's going to come back home, whether he wants to or not."

I took note of how beautiful she was as I watched her talk. She was fighting for her family, which was the same thing I had done. Only I meant it. Nina was a woman scorned, one that would say absolutely anything to break up the new foundation that Carlos and I had built.

"He's not over me, though," she continued, snapping me out of my thoughts. "He'll never let me go. That's why I had his cell phone and called you from it while he was sleeping. Hard. After I put this pussy on him. He's used to me following him around from state to state. This isn't anything new. He thrives on the drama. Loves it."

While she kept talking, I wondered why I had allowed her to continue. I would have dragged this girl up and down this food court by now, but something in me wouldn't let me. Maybe it had to do with the gypsy's prediction of love. Maybe it was my desire to actually be in love but I knew that he was the one. Yeah, one week was no time to get to know someone, but he had already proved himself by murdering my ex. So, she couldn't be telling the truth.

"I can prove it," she said. "Come with me back to my hotel. He'll be meeting me there in a couple of hours, after the concert, to talk. To make up for his abuse, like he always does. To give me a portion of the little bit of money he made. You can be hiding in the closet. To listen. To know for a fact that this isn't your man. That he misses me. That he's coming back home, and you can let go before this gets ugly."

My mind was stuck on the words *the little bit of money he made*. "He makes a lot of money. I know personally. I watched him splurge on me."

She laughed, then shook her head. "Chick, it's all a game. And you're obviously slow. He's spending his bosses' money."

"He *is* the boss!" I snapped. I threw my hand in her face. Simply didn't want to hear any more lies. I wasn't stupid. She was trying to manipulate my mind.

"I just want my husband back," Nina blurted

out. "I want you to see that he still wants me, too."

I didn't respond.

We both stared at each other strangely, wanting the same man. Like me and Oshyn had done not too long ago.

"Fine. I'll go," I agreed.

Nina smiled, rubbed her hands together, and said, "Let the games begin."

20

Chloe

Another hotel.

This time Nina's.

I sat secretly, Indian style, with my mouth shut, in the darkness of her hotel closet. Like a fucking kid in nursery school, I sat with the double doors shut tightly. The crack between the doors was my only connection to what was going on in the room. Every now and then I could see Nina prance past me half naked, wearing a black lace V-string thong with a matching bra. It was killing me not being in control. Not being in the mix. She looked good, good enough to eat, but I wasn't ready to go back to my lesbian days just yet. Besides, my instructions were to wait for Carlos to arrive. I tapped my fingers on the closet floor, becoming more impatient by the minute. I couldn't wait for that nigga to show up, so I could either blast him or prove to Nina that she was wrong about my man. It was official. I *was* in love and was ready to admit it to the world. But I didn't take too kindly to relationship betrayal. For both of their sakes, hopefully, Nina was wrong.

Time seemed to pass slowly, but when I checked the time on my cell, it read 4:00 p.m. So, on the real, things were moving rather quickly. I knew I had to get back to Oshyn, but I had already decided Carlos was equally important. Nina had R. Kelly's old tunes playing throughout the room via her iPod speaker. The song "12 Play" had just come on, sending me into a frenzy. I sang the lyrics, getting aroused second by second. I sang to myself and watched Nina as best I could as she swayed sexily across the floor. If I didn't know better, I would've thought she was purposely trying to tease me.

Her body was incredible. Sculpted like Michelangelo had created her himself. Her figure was deceiving underneath her clothing, but after seeing her in just her bra and panties, I was willing to bet she lifted light weights. I wasn't sure what else she did, but I knew I had to break free from my temporary hiding place.

I just wanted to feel her breasts.

In my mouth.

I stood up boldly, broke through the closet

doors, and walked right up on Nina, grabbing her by her hair. She looked surprised, almost wanting to ask me my reason for not hiding anymore.

"Damn, you're sexy," I told her.

I expected a response but got an unexpected advance in return. Then it happened. Her delicate lips touched mine as she pulled me close to her perky 36C breasts. It was a feeling that I had never felt with a man. No nigga on the streets could do what she was doing to me. My feelings started going wild, my thoughts first, then my hormones. Nina, on the other hand, kept her focus by driving her tongue inside my mouth, then encircling my lips artfully with her tongue.

Her artistic talent started at the top, with my lips; then she made her way down to my belly button, where she stopped and pulled my tunic shirt above my head. I played the submissive role and let her do her thing. I knew Carlos was on the way, but I was a selfish bitch. If I could sneak an orgasm and then tell him nothing happened, that worked for me. I wasn't sure what Nina had up her sleeve, but I wanted to get licked. Eaten out, like people did when eating watermelon at family reunions.

I guess I threw her off guard when I reached down, unzipped my own pants, and pulled them off, along with my thong. She smiled, then stepped back to size me up. My bra was the only garment left, and it didn't matter, since Nina had gone full steam ahead. A sense of newness filled me as she pushed me onto the bed and spread my legs apart in a wide V. Without hesitation she dove inside, headfirst, making love to my clit.

As she licked, sucked, and spat, my muscles contracted. It felt so damn good. "Damn, Nina," was all I could say. I wanted to scream but tried hard to hold it inside. Before I knew it, she started this thing where she kept flicking her tongue like a snake. The kind you want in your home. The kind you want in your bed. "Oh, shit!" I belted, then ground my ass all in her face. "Eat this pussy, Nina. It's yours. It's yourssss," I told her, prolonging the sound of the letter *s*.

I started rubbing my hands all over the top part of her head, the farthest I could reach, until she pushed me farther up the bed and drilled her tongue inside my hole. I started moaning, and my eyeballs rolled up into my head. The time had come.

Then came the knock.

The knock at the door that we both had been waiting for.

Abruptly Nina stopped. I grabbed the bitch by the ear, dragging her back down toward my pussy. She pushed me away as if she were a victim. And I was holding her hostage to bless my clit.

"Later," she told me, with a seductive grin.

"I want you to see Carlos in action. You gotta stop believing niggas," she warned.

Pissed off, I retreated to the closet and closed the door behind me. I had forgotten my shirt on the floor near the foot of the bed, but I didn't give a good fuck. My hormones were raging, and I needed to cum. Bad.

Nina's nasty ass had made it to the door and had let Carlos in by the time I had calmed myself down. I couldn't see him at first but could only hear his voice. I knew the room smelled like pussy, and wondered if he smelled it, too. Typical nigga, he just walked around, sniffing, then took his shoes off.

I jumped back and placed my hand on my heart at the thought of him getting comfortable. I expected him to be beefing with Nina or asking her why she'd called him there. Instead, Nina jump-started the conversation.

"I've been waiting for you, sexy," Nina said seductively.

"Man, Nina, you bipolar. Sometimes we friends. Other times you don't wanna even talk to me."

"That's not true, Los," she told him and placed her hands around his shoulders. I was pissed. Thought that was my pet name exclusively for me and him to use. Nina began to massage him, standing almost two feet lower than him. "You know the relationship between us has been rough lately. But just know that I still love you."

The nigga grinned. "You do?" he questioned.

"I do. In spite of everything. I wanna prove it to you," she added.

His eyes grew to the size of an eight ball. "Like we fucking?" he asked.

"Of course. You think I did all this for nothing?" Nina asked as she pranced around, modeling for my man. Her husband.

Carlos wasted no time.

"Dirty muthafucka," I said under my breath. I had my fist balled up while I watched him set the Guinness world record for the fastest man to undress.

Before I knew it, he had scooted up behind Nina and said, "You know we got to use a condom. I got one in the front pocket of my pants."

"Get it, nigga," she said, her words accompanied by the crinkling of her forehead.

Ass-naked Carlos slid the condom on, and before it was secure, it popped open. Ignoring the fact that the condom had broken, he peeled the remaining pieces off, threw them on the floor, and grabbed Nina from behind. He took a few baby steps, positioning himself closer to the bed, almost wanting to place himself for the actual fuck fest. Pulling her tightly, he yanked her with force until her ass sat firmly against his stiff dick. Carlos commenced kissing the back of her neck, while my blood continued to boil. Nina was right. *Another nigga bites the dust.* I wasn't about to let the lovebirds fuck. At least if the relationship was over, I wanted to get mine.

I opened the doors to the closet slowly, expecting Carlos to turn my way. Unfortunately for him, he was so in the Nina zone that he never looked behind him. His firm ass stared me in the face, and I wished I had a knife at that moment. I sucked it up and made my move.

I came up behind him, saying, "I'm so glad you could make it, Carlos."

He heard my voice and, without turning around, mumbled, "Chloe?"

"Yes, it's me, nigga," I said in the softest voice I could muster.

"What . . . what . . . what . . ."

"Cat got your tongue, nigga? It was just on Nina's neck. And hers was just on my pussy."

He couldn't respond.

Nina couldn't, either.

She was probably wondering why I had defaulted on the plan. That was what I did. Never followed the rules. She was also probably thinking about the consequences, what Carlos would put on her since he knew she had to be the one to let me in. I removed my bra, the only piece of clothing between us all, and threw it across the bed.

We all stood in a single-file line, naked, Carlos behind Nina and me behind him. He was still in a state of trauma. And this was made clear by the way his dick went limp. I continued to stay in line, grabbing him around the waist and resting my head on his back. I couldn't see his eyes but could tell he didn't know what to do. The nigga had been caught ready to stick his dick in Nina. But I wasn't about to let that happen. He would fuck me. And Nina would make me feel good, too. I knew she was down. The horny expression on her face showed it.

"Since you want to fuck, Carlos, how about we all fuck?" I asked him boldly.

Stunned, his voice cracked. "You . . . sure . . . Chloe?"

I'm positive," I said, moving from behind him and rushing over to rub Nina along the crack of her ass.

She smiled, showing her approval, and commenced massaging my tits. Carlos's expression spoke his feelings. He was stunned but ready and willing. Wide-eyed, he tugged at his shit, hoping to get it to its ten inches again.

"I'm fucking him first," Nina declared.

"Says who?" I bent quickly to lick his shit like a lollipop, while Nina tasted the crack of my ass. It was a threesome and a competition all in one. "Oh, no, the hell you not," I told her after tasting the appetizer.

I stood straight up, ready to ride Carlos, but Nina was already on it. She ordered Carlos to sit and within seconds went to work on his knob. She slobbered and slobbered, while

Carlos reared back, with his hands gripping the comforter on the bed. Nina had her knees on the floor, while I positioned myself on the floor and commenced licking her clit. I kept teasing her . . . stopping, then starting again. Besides, I was envious of the way she made my man moan. Jealousy traveled through my veins as my nose began to spread.

I wasn't having it and couldn't play along. I hopped up, knocked Nina out of the way, and threw myself onto the bed. I rolled onto my back and cocked my legs high in the air, staring at Carlos with a threatening look. He knew what time it was. Within seconds, he had hopped onto the bed and onto my sweaty body. He thrust himself into my wetness like I was the only woman on earth, causing me to forgive the fact that he was gonna fuck Nina.

The nigga was working me overtime, trying to cram every ounce of dick up in me. He ground hard, and I pushed back as he dug deeper. At that moment, the bitch Nina got clever. She rushed us out of nowhere, sitting on her knees right beside Carlos. Before I knew it, she'd arched her back and positioned her neatly shaven pussy directly in Carlos's line of sight.

"Eat it," she begged.

He took one lick, ready to feast, until I yanked at his arms, showing my resistance. I couldn't believe that while he was on top of me, working my walls, she wanted to steal the show. A showstopper Nina would not be. I was the only bitch who could do shit like that.

I changed shit up.

I pressed against Carlos's chest, signaling him to get off of me. It was my turn to ride. Nina was still on her knees, looking at me like a pitiful child. I smiled at her, then kissed her ferociously on the mouth. I saw Carlos slide under me, showing me that he knew what was up. I wanted him on his back for me to take control. Suddenly, I rammed his stiff dick inside of me and started riding him slowly at first. Nina had me mesmerized by the way she switched up her flow. She remained on the bed, still on her knees, biting at my hardened nipples and French-kissing me in the mouth.

My movements on top of Carlos quickened as I felt an orgasm heading to the surface. I started bucking like a disgruntled bull, asking him to give me more.

"More, more!" I shouted while working my pussy on his thick dick.

I pushed my shit as far as it would go onto Carlos's manhood. I wanted to explode but had some more riding to do. Hours, if possible. My chances of Carlos holding out for me to get my nut off were slim. The nerves in his dick jumped like crazy as Nina kept encircling my nipples with her tongue. We were fucking like jackrabbits, calling out over the music in the room.

Then it happened.

Nina had something to say. Her face was balled up and had turned a bright reddish color.

"Chloe, one thing I forgot to tell you."

I just looked at her real crazy like. Wondering what made her think I would stop, or even rise up off the dick.

"Carlos has AIDS," she told me wickedly.

21

Chloe

Before I was able to get his big, diseased dick out of me, Carlos grabbed Nina's throat with his strong hand, which was big enough to palm a basketball. She tried to break free, her big, pierced titties swinging around, as he choked her ferociously. And Nina struggled to suck up any available air. I watched, wishing that it was my hands that were causing her pain. Wishing it was my hands that were squeezing out all the life that was in her body. A beautiful, thick body that would go to waste in just a few seconds, like my girlfriend Joy's had only a few years ago.

Déjà vu.

Was what my life had become.

The words *Carlos has AIDS* ran across my

mind over and over again while I watched them fight.

"You fucking bitch!" he spat continuously at his wife. A woman whom he once loved. A woman whom he now despised. All her scratches and punches went unnoticed, until one of her nails caught his eye and he suddenly let go of her neck, like a wounded puppy would to tend to his injury.

She coughed.

And then gagged.

And then inhaled as much air as she could, trying to recoup all of it that had been lost.

"He didn't tell you?" she asked as she punched him in the same eye that was wounded. "He cheated on me, brought that incurable shit into my home, and into my son's life!" Tears exploded out of her eyes as she found the strength to continue. "And I forgave him. Because that's what you do for love. Because he was my husband, and because I made a vow to never leave, no matter what!"

"She's lying!" he managed to say between his constant groans. "I don't have anything!"

He continued to press his palm against his eye, somehow hoping that the pressure would take the pain away. But I was sure that it was only making the problem worse.

"You lying bastard!" she screamed after taking her foot and ramming it into his balls. "You didn't even have the balls to tell me about it yourself. You made the doctor tell me, while your bitch ass sat in the chair, crying, apologizing, because you stole my son's future from us before he was even born."

While they went on with their family issues, I slipped away to the corner of the room and put on my clothes, still trying to wrap my head around the fact that this dude had HIV and had stuck his dick inside of me raw. They continued to argue while I watched, and I was so confused and angry that I became numb.

So numb that I couldn't feel the anger that slowly began to mount in my heart. So numb that I couldn't feel the urge to murder. I had become so numb that I didn't feel myself walking over to the wide glass bottle of Patrón Platinum, picking it up, and pouring the tequila all over her naked body.

"What in the hell are you doing?" she asked as she switched her focus from her disease-riddled husband to me.

I took the lighter that sat near where the bottle of Patrón had once been and lit it. Answering her question. The dancing orange flame barely grazed her skin before it took over and met with the tequila, engulfing her in flames. The screams that escaped out of her mouth didn't even sound human as she danced around, trying her best to put the fire out.

I was not able to tell if Carlos was happy with the fact that I had finally gotten her to shut up or mad that I had gotten rid of his wife for life. He remained emotionless, that is, until she ran toward him. The sound of the fire alarm and the smell of burning flesh filled the room as she melted away, and when she reached him, he quickly kicked her away, not wanting to risk the chance of catching fire himself. Now that bitch could feel the pain I felt when I was on fire. Somebody needed to feel that pain.

The sprinkler system finally caught wind of the danger I had created in the room, and the water poured down over us. Nina's body lay on the floor as the fire died down, and Carlos threw on his clothes in record time.

"Help me" and "I love you" were words I thought I heard slip out of Nina's mouth while Carlos finished up by putting his shoes on.

"Get the fuck up and come on. We gotta get out of here!" he demanded as he quickly headed toward the door.

"You don't want to kiss her good-bye?" I asked sarcastically as I quickly followed him out.

He never answered.

Never looked behind him, to see if his other half was okay, before shutting the door on her freshly burned body.

By the time we reached his car, three fire trucks had flooded the parking lot, and the firefighters ran out of their vehicles, suited up and ready to do their jobs. Carlos had lit up a joint and began smoking it. He was obviously disturbed, as he pulled on the brown blunt unusually hard. We sat in his car in silence for several minutes, not wanting to look suspicious, until he decided to start it up. Purple haze filled the new rental car he had gotten. It didn't mix well with the new car scent that the car had.

I cracked the window.

Needed to breathe.

"What the fuck were you doing in Nina's hotel room, anyway?" Not sure why that was the first question he thought to ask, but I assumed that he had just recalled the fact that I had come out of the closet and not through the front door.

"What the fuck was I doing in there?" I repeated. "What the fuck were *you* doing in there?"

We questioned each other as if we had been a couple since adolescence. As if it hadn't been only a week since we first met. We questioned each other as if we weren't actually strangers, and I watched him scratch his head, as if he was trying to come up with an answer.

"She said that you have AIDS. AIDS!" I yelled, trying to stop the throw up that had begun to come up my throat.

"I don't have AIDS—"

"HIV, muthafucka! Don't act like you don't know what the hell I'm talking about!"

"I don't have that shit, either. I don't have anything, no STDs, nothing. That stupid-ass bitch was lying to you! She just wanted to make you mad. She just wanted to ruin my life."

I stared at him, with my gut instinct trying to warn me that the words that fell off his tongue were all lies. My instincts screamed in my ear, telling me not to trust him, telling me to kill him and get rid of the body. And then I stared at him, trying to figure out why I wanted to believe him. Trying to find the turning point in my life where my desire to be loved overrode my desire to kill. And then my mind cruised back to the words of the gypsy. A strange old woman whose words had instantly changed my life.

"I have to get the fuck out of this town," Carlos said as he inhaled the last of the thick smoke and then put out the rest of his blunt. "The money I came here to make just isn't worth it."

I thought about what Nina had told me before I spoke confidently. "Carlos, I know all about you and how you make your money. It's not even yours," I said sadly.

"Don't believe what you hear. I do have partners," he admitted. "We split the money, and it's normally good," he lied. "We've just been taking losses."

When Carlos couldn't look me in the face, I knew Nina must've told me the truth. He was probably a worker. A damn flunky. Someone I didn't want or need.

He continued to rant. "Two people have been murdered in this city that my face can be tied to. Shit that will put me away for life. I just can't risk staying here. I'm going to leave. Now!"

"What about me?" I asked, not hearing anything about *us* in his plans.

"Are you serious? Absolutely none of this shit would've happened to me if I hadn't met you. Nothing has gone right since you came in the picture. I mean, it's as if the world came tumbling down the moment I laid my eyes on you."

He said it.

Crushing the high hopes I had for us recklessly with his words.

Contradicting the fortune-telling promise I received of the true love that would come into my life. But I knew just how to solve it. He would die just like the rest of them. Just like everyone else who had hurt my heart and betrayed my trust. Carlos no longer got a pardon for being "the one," and I was going to teach him a very valuable lesson. That I, Chloe Rodriguez, wasn't meant to be fucked with.

I shifted around in my seat, the tension of stress creeping up my spine, as I began brainstorming quick ways to kill him. Although I would prefer that he die a long, torturous death, like I had planned for Oshyn, I still had my obligation to get back to her and finish her off.

She was more important.

It was personal.

"But there's something about you that won't let me leave you alone," he said, interrupting my thoughts of ending his life. "It's like we were meant to be." He drove off in a daze, in an attempt to figure everything out. He had somewhat put my mind at ease, and for the moment, his execution had been stayed. "I want you to come with me."

Elated to hear his change of heart, I once again became the schoolgirl who had her first crush. "But where would we go?" I asked, not really caring.

"It doesn't matter. I have to go get my son first, but we could move out of the country. Start over. Raise a family."

All of that sounded really good and all, but the thought of raising Nina's son as mine really left a bad taste in my mouth. The baby would be interference in my master plan and would quite possibly, at times, come first. His son would remind Carlos of his wife, and even if he didn't say it, I knew that he would miss her occasionally. A risk I couldn't take.

I would find a way to get the little bastard out of our lives permanently, even if it took killing him off. But Carlos wouldn't miss him for long, because I would give him plenty of sons of my own.

And a daughter.

Just one.

And we would raise our family just as Brooklyn and Oshyn did. In another country. Making money illegally somehow. I began to tingle with joy at the mere thought of finally being someone's wife, and I would protect my family until my death. Not like Oshyn had done by letting me kill them all off. But she was no one to be compared to. She had always been a scared-ass bitch. Never had balls. Always borrowed mine.

"You don't have to bring anything," he said as he jumped on the highway. "I'm going to go straight to the city now, pick li'l man up, and we can book a flight from there."

This dude has it all planned out, I thought as I admired his ability to think ahead. And then it hit me. Like a ton of bricks.

"I can't go right now. I just have one more thing to do. Let's leave first thing in the morning, okay?"

"One more thing? We'll be in jail *before* first thing in the morning comes, and going by your fucking track record, someone else will be dead."

And oh, how right he was.

Oshyn was still a priority, and I needed to go back and finish the business I had started with her and the kids before I left town. Although I wanted to make her torture long and painful, with the new plans, I was going to have to speed it up if I wanted to squeeze the kids in with it. There were no ifs, ands, or buts about it. The deed had to be done before I left for Rochester, New York.

"This is important. If this is my last time here, I have to finish this. Turn this car around, and take me back to my car," I said, remembering that it was still in the hotel parking deck.

"Don't you ever watch the movies? All the major kingpins got caught because they had to make one more move before they quit the drug game forever. Their one more move always landed them with a life sentence or death. I can't risk that. I'm not turning around."

As much as I wanted a chance at raising my own family, my desire to get revenge for everything Oshyn had done to me was bigger. An addiction that I was sure would lead to my demise, but it was a risk I was willing to take. I grabbed the steering wheel, which he had such a tight hold on, and yanked it to the left, causing the car to swerve into the next lane. The other drivers honked their horns repeatedly.

"What the fuck are you doing, stupid bitch!" Carlos yelled.

"Take me back to my car!" I screamed like I was going insane. "Take me back now!" I warned one more time before I yanked the wheel again, this time causing the car to go over the grates that made all that noise.

He slapped me so hard, he knocked me back on my side of the car.

Where I originally was.

Where I was originally supposed to be.

And just as he was about to swing on me again, sirens went off behind us. An unmarked black Charger was the cause of all the racket, and with all the swerving our car had done into other lanes, and the sweet smell of weed that still lingered in the air, I couldn't think of any other choice but to run.

22

Chloe

"Oh shit, look what *you* did!" Carlos said, panicking. His foot never let up on the pedal as I watched the dial on the speedometer rise to one hundred miles per hour.

"Me?" I asked as I pressed my hand roughly against my chest. "How the fuck is any of this my fault?"

"You should've kept your hands to yourself. If you hadn't taken the steering wheel and jerked the car around, the police wouldn't be in back of us now. It's broad daylight out here. What in the hell were you thinking? It's your fault that they're behind us. If it's not one thing, it's the next fucking with you!"

I turned around and noticed that another police car, this one marked, had decided to join the party. He was trailing behind the unmarked Charger, and both were keeping a steady speed behind us.

"It's like you have a curse on you or something," he added as he rolled down his window, trying to get the scent of the purple haze out of the car. As if that was going to stop the inevitable.

His arrest.

He was now tipping over one hundred and ten miles per hour, and if nothing else, they were going to arrest him for running from the law, which was something I had done all my life. And got away with. Paranoia had replaced his high as he struggled to come to terms with the fact that this might be the end for him.

"I can't even fucking believe that I got caught up with a bitch like you. You ruined my whole life. My whole fucking life!"

I sat in my seat and soaked in all his words. *This muthafucka doesn't even realize how lucky he really is,* I thought as I desperately began wishing that I got the chance to show him how I really got down.

"I can't believe that the police—"

"Shut the fuck up about them! Believe me, if you knew how a bitch like me got down, you would know that they are the least of your worries."

"Who do you think you're talking to? You shut the fuck up before I knock all the teeth out of your mouth like Nina. And you know what? As a matter of fact, when all of this blows over, I'm going to beat the shit out of you."

"Do you know who you're dealing with? Do I look like your bitch-ass wife?" I asked before punching him on the side of his face. He took one hand off the steering wheel, and before he had a chance to raise it in an attempt to strike me back, I warned him about our company.

"I'm going to kill you," was what he grumbled under his breath as he rubbed his jaw and lowered his hand back on the wheel.

I remained calm, because in all actuality, I had no other choice. Any other reaction from me would've been deadly for him and fatal for my future, so I had to stay in a place where I was going to make decisions that were going to get me safely out of this car and back to Oshyn.

Carlos continued to worry and complain as I kicked myself in the ass, wondering what had made me detour from my initial mission. While I was in the hospital, recovering from Oshyn and Brooklyn's attempts to end my life, the only thoughts that ran through my mind were of her demise. I just couldn't figure out how I had let a random nigga slip in and take me off of my game. This was the second time in my life where I had been a sucka for love. I hit myself on the forehead, vowing to never let that happen again.

"You gotta be kidding me," he said suddenly.

"What?"

"There's not enough gas. I'm running out of gas!" Carlos said in a panic as he pointed to the gas light, which had just lit up. He banged his head violently on the wheel while he spat out a few more curse words. "How could I have forgotten to get the fucking gas?"

I chuckled.

Inappropriate.

Long.

Awkward.

My laughter was so out of place that even he was lost for words concerning its cause, but there was a reason for my strange outburst.

I laughed to keep myself from going insane. To stop myself from thinking that I'd never get to finish Oshyn off, and that there was a possibility that she would live longer than today all because his stupid ass didn't have enough gas in the tank to get away.

Who did that dumb shit?

On a high-speed chase?

And then I thought that maybe he was right. Maybe I was cursed and the dust that the gypsy blew on me had solidified my downfall, promising to make everything I put my hands on crumble. But I quickly dismissed the idea, because shit never went right in my life, starting with my mother, whom I missed dearly. It was at that very moment that I realized that the curse didn't come from the old, scary-looking woman in Saint-Tropez. It came from my family.

A generational curse.

That was alive and strong in me.

"I'm gonna have to pull over," he confessed as bullets of sweat began to pop out of his pores.

"For what? You have about forty more miles until the car actually stops running. The gas light is just a warning sign. Just make a couple sharp turns and lose their asses," I said, wishing that a little common sense would hit him in the head.

"Nah, that's too risky. We're going to tell the police that you were in an accident and we had to get you to the hospital for an emergency. A heart attack. When we pull over, tell the cops that you thought you were having a heart attack."

"You have to be the stupidest person alive!" I replied as I listened to the explanation that he thought was going to get him off. "A heart attack? Really? Who is going to believe that nonsense? And even if they did, we passed two hospitals already."

I rolled my eyes at his foolish idea. An idea that I wasn't going to follow through with even if it did make sense, because I was getting out of this mess. I couldn't risk not being believed by the police and being taken into custody for something as little as questioning.

Today Carlos would be left on his own.

Like I had been all my life.

"Just . . . just go with the story. That's all *we* have is this story. And you . . . ," he said, turning his head to look at me. "You owe me!"

I rolled my eyes about him using the word *we,* and I rolled them even harder at his assumption that I owed him anything. I had paid my debts to this fucked-up society and didn't owe anyone a muthafuckin' thing.

"Did you hear me?" Carlos asked in response to my silence. He took his foot off the gas, slowing down the speed of the car tremendously, and repeated himself. "Did . . . you . . . fucking . . . hear . . . me?"

"Yes, baby, I heard you," I answered back as I reached over and placed my hand on his damp thigh. A place where his stream of perspiration had also found its way to.

He looked at me with a hint of unsettlement in his eyes as he wondered why I had all of a sudden become nice. Gentle.

"I don't know how we met, and I don't even know why we met, but none of this was by chance," I said. "The one week that we have gotten to know each other feels like we've been in a ten-year relationship. It's as if we're glued together. A lot of chances to just walk away from each other have come and gone, where we would never see each other again, but we chose to stay."

I paused to let my words sink in as I watched

his heavy breathing calm down. "I'm a ride-or-die bitch, and I'm going to stick with you no matter what happens. We're going to make it out of this, and I want to be by your side when we do."

I felt the tension in his body soften up, while my sweet nothings in his ear soothed his mind, reassuring him that everything was going to be okay. When the car slowed down to about twenty miles per hour, we heard the grates sing as he eased it into the pull-over lane.

And then it stopped.

Abruptly.

For the first time since the whole ordeal began, my heart started to race. Just the mere thought of none of this working out was enough to make me throw up. *This can't be it,* I thought to myself as I caught a glimpse of the three officers walking toward us, all with their guns drawn. *This can't be how my life is supposed to end.*

"Just stay calm," he reminded me with a slight smile painted on his face, trying to convince me that everything was going to be okay. Something he couldn't guarantee himself.

"Put your hands on the steering wheel!" was what came pounding out of one of the officers' mouths as they reached the car. "And don't you move, fucker, or I'll blow your damn head off!" I knew that that wasn't proper procedure, but the police around here did whatever they wanted to do, anyway. That was just how shit was.

"Officer, I can explain," Carlos cried as he switched his demeanor from a hood nigga to . . . one of them. "Please, it's an emergency. My girlfriend thinks that she is having a heart attack. She has a bad heart, and I need to get her to the hospital as soon as possible. I couldn't afford to stop for you guys, because I just didn't want her to die."

"That doesn't make any sense, because you just sped past two hospitals before pulling over here," one of the officers pointed out.

"Yeah, but I'm not from here and I was in a panic. She wasn't talking, but now that you mention it, I recall her pointing several times, trying to get me to see something, but I just had no idea what to do. There was so much confusion. You all were following me. I'm not a criminal. She was dying. . . . I just didn't know what to do. I still need to get her to the emergency room, though. Time is of the essence."

I had to admit it. Carlos was good, so good that the officers' aggressiveness had simmered down a little bit. So good that I grasped my heart to see if there was still a steady beat, and worried when it seemed to pound rapidly. So good that for the first time, I thought that we had a good chance of getting out of this mess.

"Please, Officer, you can lead the way so we can get there faster, and I can give you all my information when we arrive, but we can't just sit here. We have to get her some kind of help."

He took my hand and squeezed it, assuring me again that he had everything all under control.

"Ma'am," another officer said as he tapped on my window, "can you please roll this window down?"

I followed his instructions and pressed the button that sat on the armrest. A nice breeze floated from outside and grazed my cheekbone as the man with the badge looked at me with sympathy.

"Are you okay?" he asked.

I ignored him.

Looked forward, as if he wasn't speaking to me. As if our lives didn't depend on a simple yes or no answer.

"Ma'am, I just asked you a question. Are you okay?" I could tell by his voice that the ease he once had had quickly slipped away as he placed his fingers on the unlatched gun that sat on his hip.

"Baby, answer him. Tell him the truth, that everything is *not* okay and that you need to get some help *now*. Tell him what he wants to hear," Carlos pleaded with me, worried about the fact that I was going to fuck up the masterpiece he had just created.

And he was right.

I couldn't risk his master plan not working,

and no matter how close we seemed to be to freedom, it just wasn't close enough. Just the thought of me not being able to feel this breeze was intolerable.

"No, I'm not okay," I responded. Carlos breathed a sigh of relief as I continued. "I'm being held against my will! I'm not having a heart attack, but he told me that he would kill me if I didn't play along!"

"You stupid bitch!" Carlos screamed as my body served as a punching bag for his heavy punches.

"Help me!" I screamed, and it took all the officers to pull him off of me. "He killed him. He's the guy that murdered that man at the funeral home, and he set his wife on fire at the Ramada Inn on Jefferson Road not even twenty minutes ago."

"She's lying!" Carlos belted, trying his best to break the hold they had on him. "That bitch is a fucking liar!"

"I tried to get away. Tried to call you all for help, but he wouldn't let me. I saw what he did. Twice. I watched how he set the woman he promised to love and cherish on fire and she went up in flames, and I believed him when he said that he would do the same to me."

Tears poured out of my eyes as one of the officers pulled me to the side in an attempt to console me. Even with his handcuffs on, the other officers continued to tussle with Carlos, as he proved that he wasn't going to give up without a fight. The guy that sat by my side excused himself to help his colleagues, and I was left alone.

Leaning against Carlos's car.

With the key still in the ignition.

When I felt like everyone was engrossed in calming down their suspect in two unsolved murders, I ran to the driver's side of the car, opened up the door, and jumped in.

"Hey, stop . . . ," was all I heard as I cranked up the ignition and drove away, with just enough gas to get me to the place that was most important. To the place I had had no business leaving in the first place. Back to Oshyn, where I belonged.

23

Oshyn

"Mommy . . . Ma . . . wake up!"

His voice had changed, and he was beginning to sound like a young man. As if he had had one of those dreams that transformed boys into men overnight and had woken up wet.

"Mom, I said, wake up!"

I slowly opened up my eyes and was greeted by my firstborn son, Micah, who showed nothing but teeth as he smiled at me. His presence was warm. His touch missed.

I let the word *Micah* slip out of my mouth as I brushed my finger along his soft chocolate face. "Mommy missed you so much."

"I missed you, too," he admitted as he giggled innocently. "Come with me." He grabbed my hand and began leading me into the light.

I took a few steps and then slowed down, until I stopped. "Come on!" he demanded as his strong little hands tugged on mine a little bit harder.

"Wait, where are you taking me?"

"With me," he answered, with a bit of an attitude. Very defensive, like I should've known the answer to my own question. Like I should not have questioned him at all.

"Baby, you have to tell me where you're going. Where does that light lead to?" I shielded my eyes from its brightness.

He looked down.

Never answering my question.

"You are *my* mommy. You *have* to come and live with *me* now!" He had begun to pout, as children so selfishly do.

"Where are Mye and Bella?" I asked curiously, wondering why I didn't see them anywhere around.

Micah and Bella were best friends, soul mates. The kind that would've gotten married when they were only in their twenties. I just found it odd that he was without her. And I was sure that his little brother, Mye Storie, whom he had never met before, would be in his arms. Showing him the ropes of life, as big brothers do, but the kids weren't there.

Just him.

And I found that odd.

"Micah, where are Bella and Mye?" I asked again.

"Who cares? You're with me now, and we're together again. They don't matter anymore. Come on!"

He pulled my arm harder than before, refusing to let me disappear out of his life once again. My prince had become so determined.

"I can't go with you, baby. Mommy loves you, but I just can't go. It's not my time," I confessed as it finally sunk in as to where I was. The afterlife.

"But what about me?" he whined as he started to cry. Despite his deepened voice, he was still too young to understand the choice that I had to make.

I kneeled down to kiss him on the forehead and then wrapped him in my arms. "Please understand. I know it's hard, but your aunt Chloe is trying to hurt them really, really bad. I have to save them. I have to stop her."

He held on tighter, ignoring my pleas for help. Ignoring my pleas to allow me to save a life. He didn't care, because no one had saved his. We cried together as we embraced.

"I have to go now," I said.

His grip got tighter.

Suffocated me.

"Micah, I have to go," I repeated.

He wouldn't listen.

Closed his eyes tighter.

"Let me go!" I said forcefully as I pried his arms from around me. It took a while for me to get them off, but I finally did, and before I thought twice, I turned around and walked away.

From the light.

And my son.

I couldn't bear to look at his face a moment longer. Couldn't bear to witness the sadness that lived in his eyes, because I might have changed my mind and stayed.

"I love you," were the last words I said before I entered complete blackness.

"Where am I?" I asked as I came to.

I was greeted by a painfully pounding head and a constant flickering movement that seemed to be stuck in my mind, the taste of blood staining my tongue, and a burning feeling on the corner of my eye and lip.

I was fucked up.

I looked around and saw the steel table that housed all the items that I had initially put together to kill her with, but she had overpowered me and was now in control. However, she was nowhere around.

"Help, help . . . help . . . help!" I screamed into the empty warehouse as I listened helplessly while the echoes bounced off the walls. "Help!"

No answer.

Not that I expected one.

My hands were still tied together, and I tried

my best to unravel the rope, but nothing seemed to work.

"Mama . . . I need you!" I waited for her to come. "Mama, please, tell me what to do!"

No answer.

This surprised me.

I started to cry, feeling like there was nothing that could be done. I was beginning to lose hope, which didn't matter, because I had lost everything else. Hope was, at this point, just a privilege I had gotten used to not having.

"Brooklyn? Micah? Anyone? Help me!"

My cries for help and heavy sobs fell on deaf ears and echoing walls, which didn't comfort me. *It's all over,* a voice whispered in my ears, loud enough to drown out the roaches' activity. *She has the kids, and they're dead. It's all over. Just give up.*

An image of the kids' dead bodies ran across my mind as my cries turned into hyperventilation. Despite the blood that saturated Mye's body, he looked to be asleep, while Bella just lay there with her eyes open, startled. As if she'd fought. Hard.

"I'm going to kill you!" I screamed to no one in particular, but directing all of my rage to Chloe. "I'm going to kill you!"

I lowered my head in defeat as I let the words "God help me" slither out of my mouth. A name I hadn't called before. It was the only name that could rescue me, and instantly a peace and calmness came over me that was so strong I was in awe. The running cockroaches in my ears came to a halt, and the excruciating pain in my head that I was experiencing stopped. Nothing seemed to make sense, and everything had all of sudden become okay.

I realized that if I didn't switch my thinking I was going to die, and that was not the position I wanted to be in. Even though I had a million reasons why I wanted to be dead, I had two reasons to live. God had let me know that they were okay, and that was the voice I chose to listen to.

I wiggled the rope that remained tied around my wrists some more, until they became tender. Sore, even. I was getting rope burn, but that was the least of my worries. At this point, anything was better than the silence of death. You couldn't wake up from that.

Ten minutes passed as I worked relentlessly to get my wrists loose, and just when I was about to give up, I hit a turning point and the rope loosened. Not enough for me to get my hands free, but enough to sustain the hope I was trying so hard to hold on to. *Just a few more minutes,* I said to myself. *I just need a few . . . more . . . minutes.* I worked vigorously to get the rope off. Even though my skin had become raw, I refused to give up.

But I didn't have a few minutes.

"Oh no," I whispered to myself. I stopped what I was doing when I heard keys clanging together in the not too distant hallway. She was back, and I wasn't prepared. Unable to try any longer, I stopped all movement and lowered my head back down and closed my eyes. I needed for her to think that I was still unconscious.

"Oshyn, my dear," she sang out sarcastically. "You have no fucking idea what it took to get me back to you. I almost didn't make it. I got my pussy sucked, set the bitch that did it on fire, and was in a police chase before it was all over!"

With my eyes closed, I listened intently as her feet shuffled around some more.

"Me killing your ass must be meant to be."

She laughed.

Passionately.

Arrogantly.

"Oshyn!"

I slowed my breathing a bit so she couldn't tell that I had been active. The last thing I needed was for her to think that I had been awake, trying to break out of here.

"Oshyn!"

As her footsteps got closer, I closed my eyes tighter, trying to prepare myself for the worst. I was certain that the longer I held out on answering her, the more that upped my chances of sustaining another blow to my head.

And I was right.

The massive pain of her banging me on the top of my head was so bad that I had been paralyzed by fear. My head hurt so bad that any exhaling and inhaling I did made me tremble. So I stopped and held my breath for as long as I could.

"Oshyn!" she screamed for the third time, and before she could hit me again, I looked up. Slowly. Showing her I was weak and vulnerable. "Good morning, sister. . . . So glad that you could finally join us today. I have to admit it, I sort of didn't think you were going to come to after I left, but hallelujah, you made it through!"

The enthusiasm in her voice disgusted me, as I heard in her voice how happy she was that she had another chance to kill me. All the laughter immediately died down when she asked, "Where are Mye and Bella?"

That was a question I just wasn't going to answer. I kept my mouth closed as I watched her walk to the table and grab the bottle of acid that I had brought to use on her. She had turned my own weapons of mass destruction on me.

"Sulfuric acid," she read off the white container. "Now, this is going to be fun!" She twisted off the top and walked back over to me. "I'm going to ask you again. . . . Where are Mye and Bella?"

"Chloe, please, just leave them alone. They're just children, and they have nothing to do with this shit. Your beef is not with them. It's with me."

"Oh, but you're wrong. My beef is with you and everybody that you love. I want you to feel the pain that I've felt all my life and—"

"Look at me!" I screamed, trying to bring her back into reality. "Just fucking look at me! Doesn't it look like I feel what you feel? You took everyone I had. Everyone that has ever loved me. You've murdered them. You have hurt me more than you can ever imagine. We're even!"

"No. I haven't killed everyone. When I get your raggedy-ass kids good and dead, then my mission will be complete."

"Please . . . just leave them out of this," I cried out again, hoping she would have mercy on me and hear my pleas.

"Do you know what sulfuric acid does to you?" she asked, quickly changing the subject. She poured a little of it into the bucket of water she'd tried to drown me in, and it started to boil. "If this is what it does to water, what do you think it will do to that soft, supple skin of yours?"

She waited for my response.

I said nothing.

"The kids will dissolve away in no time once I pour this over them."

"If you fucking touch those kids, I will . . ."

"You'll what?" She chuckled. "I don't believe that you're in any position to make idle threats now, are you?"

I wasn't.

Mye and Bella were still in the hotel room, safe for the moment with my grandmother, but I didn't know how long that was going to last. I couldn't imagine them being put in the foster care system if Chloe ended up winning the battle and killing me. And then the thought of the state finding the last family member left, Chloe, and giving her physical custody made me sick.

Nauseous.

"I'm going to ask you one more time. Where are those kids?"

I stood my ground and remained defiant as she walked up to me, close enough for me to smell the scent of sex and death that rested on her skin. She raised the bottle and smiled. "Fine. Have it your way. Open wide. . . ."

24

Chloe

Driving crazily.
Adrenaline pumping.
Hoping to kill within minutes.

I pushed aside any concern I had for the police while dodging in and out of traffic. I had already made it past Broadway and was racing down State Street. Feeling like my future was on the line, I thought long and hard about how I would handle things when I got to the hotel. Bella, of course, would be killed. There were no other options. She had ruined my life for the past two years and needed to be taken out. Mye, I wasn't sure. . . . His fate had possibilities. I could just shoot him—two blanks to the head—or maybe even take him to his mother and kill them both together.

Before I could even bring myself to focus

on Oshyn's date with death, my phone rang. It was a Raleigh area code, yet the number didn't ring a bell with me. I wondered who would be calling me at a time like this. As I turned the corner sharply, I answered with bass in my voice.

"Yeah," I spat.

The voice was frail and weak and unrecognizable as the person spoke softly into the phone.

"Tommy, is that you?" I was clearly irritated.

"Chloe, I . . . I . . . I . . . I . . . need to see you," he struggled to say.

"Tommy, I gotta call you back later. I'm handling something right now." The tone of my voice should've been a sign that I couldn't talk, but he insisted.

"Chloe, there may not be a later," he informed me sadly. "You gotta sign one more paper that I forgot about."

A lump formed in my throat, and I instantly got wet. Visions invaded my head of me in all black, with a big, wide hat, and tons of people giving me their condolences. Most of all, I had his money. All of it.

"Chloe, do you hear me?" Tommy asked in his fragile voice. "The lawyer said it has to be signed."

"Yeah, I hear you. I'll fly out tomorrow."

"No, Chloe," he pleaded. "The latest . . . the latest, the latest," he kept saying.

I became irritated. "The latest what?"

"The latest is now. . . . It's very bad. I could go at any time." He struggled to get his words out clearly. "The doc said things don't look so good. I've taken a turn for the worse."

"A turn for the worse?" I questioned as a mini grin slipped through the side of my lips.

"This is the best I've felt all day. But who knows."

Tommy began to cry like a bitch. A weak man on his deathbed was always beyond pitiful, but I listened, anyway, as I took the exit ramp, planning to make a U-turn to head to the airport. He kept talking while I made plans to get to Raleigh to sign the necessary paper. It would be well worth it in the end, I convinced myself.

Four hours and thirty-three minutes later, I had landed in the land of prosperity.

Raleigh, North Carolina.

A place where I used to get money.

A place full of memories.

Both good and bad.

My heels clicked along the cold floor as I pranced my way down the halls of WakeMed Hospital. As usual, all eyes were focused on me. I was tired from the plane ride, but it didn't affect my appearance much. I had stopped in the bathroom on the first floor so I could freshen up and spread some gloss on my lips for Tommy. I wanted to look good as I signed my name on the dotted line. When I got to his room, I pushed on the closed door slowly, unsure of what I would see.

The stench.

That awful hospital smell.

It all hit me as soon as the door opened. Luckily, Tommy had a spacious room, so as soon as I walked in and closed the door, I scoped out the place, trying to see where I would sleep. He had a single room, no roommate, so I wondered who the two extra people were who chatted over in the corner with the nurse in the Pooh Bear scrubs. They talked intently, using library voices, while staring me down in the process. One woman left abruptly, but not before I shot her the evilest expression I could muster. I wasn't sure if the other lady in all white was a social worker or was from the department who handled people who were about to die. I was hoping for the latter, considering Tommy looked like shit on a stick.

Without hesitation, I flew over to Tommy's bed, sat by his side, and threw my head, like a drama queen, onto his torso. I just knew he would be glad to see me. Oddly, his body didn't move. Seemed that he had no reflexes. No movement at all. At first I thought that he'd passed already, but then I felt his stomach inflating and deflating slowly. He was still alive, yet it was clear Tommy wouldn't make it much longer.

It dawned on me that I had arrived just in

time. I could've kicked myself in the ass for not watching over my jackpot more closely. By his side was where I should've been for days, instead of fooling with Oshyn and Carlos. I sat back in the chair, trying to get comfortable, then grabbed a business magazine lying on the small table next to his bed. It was called *Today's Entrepreneur*. I grabbed it, noticing Tommy was featured on the cover. The tagline read, "One man's journey to millions in the stock market." *Damn, Tommy looks decent on the cover,* I told myself, slipping the magazine into my purse to read later. I should've played him more closely, I thought. Would probably be sitting extra pretty by now.

The more I thought about my mistakes, the more I felt someone watching me. From the corner of my eye I noticed the same woman in white moving curiously in my direction. Everything was quiet, until she had the audacity to ask me who I was.

"I'm his soul mate," I said. "He called, so I came as fast as I could," I informed her, while forcing water to well up in my eyes. It was hard, and I had to think of anything that would make me cry. And so I did. It was my life. The fact that I could never find love. The fact that every person I had ever met had fucked me over. I started thinking about myself, selfishly, just as I always did when other people needed me.

I sort of tuned the woman out until she said, "I'm Ms. Stevens."

My eyes grew two times their normal size. The bitch had actually called out Tommy's last name. It was possible that she was a younger sister, perhaps even a cousin. Certainly not a secret wife that he had not told me about. Immediately, I started to drill her with questions.

"So what relation are you?"

"No, tell me more about you," she countered.

"Look, you some long-lost cousin," I began to say, but the sound of the machines going off startled us both.

We both turned our attention back to Tommy, the emotional woman rushing to the opposite side of his bed. She was a skinny, tall woman shaped like a model, with no ass at all. She wasn't too cute, if you asked me, especially with the freckle thing going on all over the middle of her face.

We both took turns rubbing his arms and trying to get him to respond to us. I needed him to be coherent so I could ask for the last paper that I had to sign. But his eyes were still glossy and half closed when I said, "Tommy, I'm here, baby. You told me to come, so I came. Where's the paper, baby?"

The nurse looked at me crazily and asked me to step back for a second. I obliged for a few seconds, until she said, "His heart rate is getting even lower. Not good."

My facial gestures showed my confusion, but it seemed the nurse and the woman knew more than I did. They were obviously in tune with one another. It was clear by the way they exchanged saddened looks, followed by deep eye contact. I just turned my attention to Tommy, who continued to lie all the way back, almost stiff like a mummy, and appeared almost incoherent. It seemed like he was waiting on death to touch him on the shoulder. His breathing had been irregular ever since I entered the room, but it was now becoming more sluggish. When I saw his eyes rolling up into his head, I touched his hand, which felt colder than ice, then made myself drop a tear.

"Tommy, I really need that paper," I whispered into his ear. "It's me, baby. I'm here," I told him, hoping for some sign.

"Rest easy. I'm here," the mysterious woman said, obviously competing with me. She began patting his forehead, trying to make his journey a comfortable one. Me, I was in a state of panic. I needed to sign on the dotted line, and Tommy was two steps from death. I didn't give a fuck about how he left the earth . . . comfy or not. I just wanted my inheritance.

"Oh, Tommy," I called out. "Don't leave me, Tommy! We've been through so much together," I moaned loudly, then grabbed his hand again. "Wake up, Tommy! Wake up!"

Suddenly, Tommy opened his eyes slightly, then mouthed a few shocking words. "Chloe, you deceived me, sweetie."

I got up close to his face and rubbed his arm, letting him know I was by his side. "Rest easy. Don't strain yourself."

"N-o-o-o, I got-t-t-ta tell you. I know the investigators came through," he confessed in a light whisper. "No daughter, no love for me . . ."

"Shhhhh," I said in a caring tone, hoping he would shut the fuck up. I swallowed hard, wondering what he meant. "But you called me, honey. I'm here. Don't worry yourself about anything else."

"Yeah . . . I called," he said, almost with a smirk. "I needed you to know that I know. . . ." It seemed he was on some get back, but I wasn't sure. The sickness had him beat, so he couldn't even finish his sentence.

Then it happened.

My demise began.

The bitch flew from the opposite side of the bed and touched me on the shoulder. "No disrespect, miss, but you really have to go."

"And who's going to make me?" I replied. I stood up, ready to buck.

"Me. I'm the next of kin," she told me firmly. "I'm his daughter, and I don't think that you're supposed to be here."

I turned my neck slowly like the crazy bitch from *The Exorcist.*

"What did you say to me? I'm Chloe Rodriquez, his woman!" I pointed at Tommy like I wanted a dying man to back me up.

"Listen, my father is dying. They expected him to be gone by now." Her voice was confrontational. "This is a private moment for us, so I'd like for you to leave us so I can say good-bye properly."

"Look," I said boldly, "I'm his beneficiary, so I should be able to say good-bye, too." I made sure to sound like I really cared. "I signed papers just days ago, so I should be able to stay just like you." I swung my eyes over to the nurse for approval.

"Listen, my father and his lawyer had those papers rescinded. I signed the new paperwork. So go," she insisted, shooing me off like a fly. "You'll never touch my father's money. Besides, he doesn't even know you. You took advantage of his illness, and he wasn't in his right mind when it happened. You won't be an Anna Nicole to my family," she added coldly.

"That's n-not tr-true," I stuttered. "He called me."

A huge smile erupted on her face when she let out her next words. "Those papers were torn to shreds. He called me right after he talked to you. Too late," she teased.

My mind was being fucked with.

Picked at.

Torn apart.

I thought Tommy had everything covered, I said to myself. Weren't the papers I signed worth anything? Wasn't there something someone could do? My mental state had been descending for several minutes, and Tommy's daughter knew it. It could've been the smoke blowing through my nose or the fire in my eyes that warned her. Suddenly I exploded.

I sprang from my space, then leaped across the room in search of Tommy's personal belongings. And in a voice not altogether steady, said, "I signed papers less than three days ago."

I got no response, so I started throwing shit that he had stored in the bottom of his closet. It was all old photos of him and his daughter, mostly from her toddler days. Before I finished, they were all scattered across the floor, and I moved to the two drawers next to his bed. Both his daughter and the nurse paid my rampage no mind, because while I tore the room apart, Tommy took his last breath.

"He's gone," the nurse said sympathetically. She acted as though I didn't exist as I rubbed up against her slightly, still pulling shit out of the drawers.

Tommy's daughter, on the other hand, showed her dislike for me differently. She quickly pulled the white sheet over her father's body, all the way up to his eyes, as if she didn't want his dead spirit to witness her next move. She then lifted the phone and asked for security.

I started shouting, "You think that shit scares

me! All I want is my money! Tommy promised me an inheritance, and I want it!"

She kept looking at me crazily, while moving closer to her father's bed. It was almost as if she was protecting him. "Did you ever love my father?" she asked me.

"What a stupid fucking question. Where's the paper?" I asked again.

She wouldn't answer. Simply smiled her victory. My instincts told me not to back down, but the two uniformed visitors at the door told me firmly that it was time to go.

25

Oshyn

She spared me.
Maybe she loved me.
For real.
I wanted to think that for once in my life
she had left without inflicting any more pain
on me, but I knew better. The acid that she
had intended to pour down my throat would
have killed me instantly, but that wasn't what
she wanted. Before leaving to go and find the
kids, Chloe changed her mind at the very last
minute. The deadly liquid would have dissolved my teeth, eaten up the lining of my
throat and esophagus, and it would have made
the blood that flowed freely through my body
boil, like it had done the water. But she didn't
want me to die just then.
I knew that the reason was that she wanted

to watch us all suffer and cry out in agony while she sat and witnessed our demise. She had no intention this time of fucking up and letting us slip away, but somewhere along the way she had made a terrible mistake. She had underestimated my determination to live. My determination to save my family, as well as my determination to wipe her off the face of this earth. I wanted her dead just as much as she wanted me dead, and now, once again, I had my chance.

With the ropes already loosened, and my flesh already raw, I continued to work effortlessly to get myself free and get to my kids before Chloe had a chance to. I was well aware of the big head start that she had on me, but I was confident that my grandmother would somehow mess up Chloe's plans. She had promised me that she would keep them safe, and I knew that she would keep her word.

I managed to wrestle and slide the rough rope off the burning skin on my hands, and I worked quickly to untie the rope that held my ankles hostage. Finally, the ropes that had been used to bind my hands and feet together lay unraveled on the floor, but as soon as I went to stand up, my legs gave out and I fell to the floor. I was weak, exhausted, and hungry. *Get up!* I said to myself as I used the concrete floor as a mattress, but I just couldn't bear to move. I had used the only ounce of energy I had left to set myself free, and now I had nothing left to give. My breaths quickly became like those of a fish out of water.

Short.

Fast.

Numbered.

I closed my eyes, wanting nothing more than to sleep all of this pain away and wake up to find that this had all been just a really bad nightmare, but I knew that I wouldn't be so lucky. This was as real as it got, and there was no amount of wishful thinking that would get me out of this mess I was in. This was my life, plain and simple.

The blackness I saw because of my closed eyes was replaced with images of Bella and Mye playing together and loving each other. Then my visions switched to images of Chloe torturing them, blood everywhere, and of them reaching out to me in fear, and when their screams came to a ceasing halt and their eyes closed, indicating that they were beginning their journey to the other side, mine opened.

Get the fuck up! I said to myself once more, actually listening this time. At an injured turtle's pace, I slowly lifted myself up and stood to my feet. I managed to begin walking to the door, and with each step I took, I gained a little bit of strength. I got out of the warehouse and to my car. After digging into my pocket to retrieve my keys, I unlocked my door, jumped in the car, and started it. I looked down at myself and realized how much blood I had on me. So much that I was soaking in it. Just from the little movement I made in the car, it was starting to look like a crime scene, too, so I pulled away, knowing that I had to drive carefully back to the hotel in order to avoid being pulled over by the police.

I had a feeling that Mye and Bella were still in the hotel room, and that my grandmother was still keeping them out of harm's way, like she had promised. My hands began to tremble uncontrollably as the thought of me walking into the room and seeing them chopped up into a million pieces crept into my mind. One thing Chloe never did was make idle threats, and she always carried out what she said she would do, so I couldn't help but think that she had kept her word.

"Ju must hurry up and get back to the hotel. The kids are in great danger if ju don't make it there soon!"

Thinking that I was alone in the car, I turned to my right and saw my grandmother sitting beside me, looking at me with a chilling stare.

"Why aren't you with them?" I asked, horrified at the fact that she was sitting here with me instead of being where she was supposed to be.

"Ju were supposed to get rid of her!" she blurted out, ignoring my question. "This is jur fault! Ju let her get away, and now she's going to kill them!"

Kill them . . . kill them . . . kill them were the words that floated around in my head as her aged voice continued to echo in my mind. Her mouth continued to move as inaudible, broken English sentences flew out of her mouth at a mile a minute, but I couldn't hear anything anymore. I just drove straight as the words *kill them* took up permanent residence in my heart.

I drove the car, not really paying any attention to the road, and was scared shitless back to reality by a host of honking horns. I had run a red light and had almost caused a massive accident, but I didn't care. I would have run it, anyway, even if I had seen it, because I needed to get to them. I was just glad that there were no police around.

My driving mimicked that of a drunk driver as I recklessly weaved in and out of traffic, no longer able to assume responsibility for my actions. I had become intoxicated with death. My pores and my breath reeked of it. Still in a daze, I drove up to the edge of a huge cemetery. With Mama still in my passenger seat, rambling on, I turned to my left and watched the tombstones breeze by me. I couldn't help but wonder if this was where they laid Brooklyn to rest, or if they would cremate his body because it was cheaper and there was no one to claim him.

Couldn't help but wonder if his spirit would come and talk to me as my grandmother's and firstborn son, Micah's did. I couldn't help but hope and wonder if God would appoint my husband as my guardian angel. I prayed that he would so that I could feel his presence in my life just one more time. The graveyard that I couldn't seem to pry my eyes from had probably now become his home, and I couldn't find it in my heart to be okay with that.

As visions of a future without my husband began haunting me, the words *kill them . . . kill them* somehow seemed to creep back in, followed by a tremendously loud bang and my chest being rammed into the steering wheel. The air bag, which had burst in my face, just as quickly deflated. I saw that I had run into the back of a police car.

Hard.

The hood of my car was now curled up, and his rear was bashed in. I had realized that he was sitting at a red light when I banged into him, and now I watched intently as he jumped out of his car.

"Ma'am, get out of the car!" he yelled harshly, obviously pissed that I had ruined his day.

"Mama! Mama!" I screamed frantically as I looked at the passenger seat where she'd once sat. "Where is my grandmother?"

The balding white officer peered into my car to look for an injured woman but found nothing.

"Ma'am, you're the only person in here."

"No, we *have* to find her. She was just here,

talking to me, and I wasn't listening. She was trying to tell me something and I stopped listening and now she's gone!" I took a look at him and noticed him slowly putting his hand on his gun.

"Where did all that blood come from? Are you hurt?" The tone of suspicion was heavy in his voice as he realized that this was more than a reckless driving charge.

I held on to the steering wheel, and with every suffocating breath I took, I could feel the bruise that was beginning to develop on my breasts. The tears began to fly out of my eyes.

My panic started to attack.

"Where are you bleeding from?"

"My children!" I hollered. "I have to get to my children! I have to save them!" I did what I could to move the air bag out of my face and tried putting the car in reverse, until I realized that it had been cut off.

"Get out of the car now!" he demanded after opening my door.

"But you don't understand. She's going to kill them," I confessed. But I quickly learned that my cries were falling on deaf ears, just as my grandmother's had fallen on my deaf ears just moments before.

The street wasn't busy, but the few travelers on it now had to find alternate routes to their destination. I had inconvenienced them. I had inconvenienced myself.

"The state will take your kids," he threatened. "Did you hear me? You will lose them, and custody will be awarded to the state or next of kin." He paused. Waited for a response. "That's it. I'm going to take you in."

As the officer, who had a thick build, stepped forward to physically take me out of the car, I reacted quickly by slamming my door shut and attempting to turn the car on one more time. This time the ignition rumbled as my vehicle decided to finally go along with my plans. I threw the gear in reverse, forcing him to jump out of the way as my car released itself from his. Although my car's appearance was bad, it still ran well enough to get me to my destination.

"Stop now!" he demanded as he ran in front of the car with his gun drawn and pointed it at me. "Stop, or I'll shoot," he warned.

But I couldn't stop.

It was either me or him, and I refused to be taken into custody. I refused to lose this battle. I threw the gear into drive, and before another threat had a chance to fly out of his mouth, I hit the gas, slamming him in between my car and his. Threats no longer came out of his mouth. Just screams that said he would be on desk duty for the rest of his life.

Stuck in my own world, I snapped out of my daze and back into reality when I realized that a few bystanders had witnessed me paralyzing a uniformed police officer. I knew I had to make my moves quickly. With him lying on my hood, I put my car in reverse again and pushed the gas until he slid onto the ground. People began to rush to his aid and sirens rang in the distant background as I put the weapon that I now drove back into drive and made my way back onto the main street, heading in the direction of the hotel before it was too late.

26

Chloe

As soon as the plane landed on New York soil, I hopped up from my seat, then barged my way to the front. People stared, pointed, and even called me names. Surely, I didn't give a fuck! A tyrant was what I had become, and I pushed them all out of my way, cursing them as I left them behind. Some complained loudly as I stepped across luggage, laptop bags, and even strollers that got in my way. I was a bitch on a mission, ready to do some serious damage.

The entire flight back to Rochester had been a nightmare for me. My head hurt like hell, as thoughts bounced through my mind. All I could think about was how I had lost out on Tommy's inheritance. My only chance at getting lump sums of money without relying on a nigga.

"His bitch-ass daughter will pay," I told myself under my breath while waiting for the cabin door to open. It was crazy how I took a chance on leaving Oshyn alone and even abandoned the idea of kidnapping Bella and Mye, all in an effort to become a millionaire mistress again. "All for nothing!" I shouted furiously.

The head stewardess shot me a funny look as I brushed up against some old woman, pushing her out of the aisle and back into her seat. I wanted it to be clear that I would be the first one out the door. Had places to go, people to see. "Turn your head, bitch!" I snapped at the young stewardess.

She was about to say something back. But just as I cupped my hand, ready to pimp slap her, the door opened, and like I'd planned, I filed out first, cutting off the woman with the small baby in front of me. Like a power walker on a mission, I jetted down the gangway, hoping to quickly get to my rental, which was parked in the daily parking lot. My walk was brisk, and I ran down every person who appeared in my path.

I had almost made it to the end of the concourse when a flat screen hanging above an open bar area caught my attention. My skin oozed with joy when I saw his face. It was Carlos, dead and center on the Channel 11 ten o'clock news. The caption read "Captured," yet I couldn't make out the words spoken by the newscaster. The television's volume was rather low, and the white folks that sat around the bar were too loud. I started to tell them all to shut the fuck up, but I wanted to relish the delight of seeing Carlos busted. "That nigga got what he deserved," I chanted under my breath. I started laughing loudly, almost in a crazy-like state. People began to stare at me, but I didn't care.

I smiled broadly while reaching into my purse in search of an Advil. *I'll take three,* I told myself as my fingers touched the bottle. Just as I pulled the bottle from my purse, my eyes refocused on the second picture that had been added to the screen.

It was a mug shot.

My mug shot.

I was now a fugitive.

Anger filled my insides as I shouted out, "Shit!"

I banged my fist against the granite countertop on the bar, saying, "Fuck, fuck, fuck!" But my words were cut short by several fingers pointing my way. Rudely, I eyed the muthafuckas ferociously, ready to step to anybody who thought they should be involved in my business. One woman looked at the screen, then at me, then back at the screen again.

And just like the perfect citizen, one older white man close to eighty had the nerve to hop up and rush over to a security guard.

With nerve, I stood in place while the older man pointed to me, then back to the TV. As he was giving his side of the story, the guard got on his walkie-talkie and called in the militia. I finally figured out I needed to move when I saw two uniformed guards walking briskly from the other end. Within seconds, I darted down the hallway, then took the escalators toward the baggage claim. I wasn't far from the entrance but could see airport security getting thicker around the outside exit and entrance areas. I had to think fast.

My eyes spotted a few unattended suitcases off to the side. Some with flowery prints, others extra ugly. But one caught my attention. It was a plain black roller bag with a huge hat sitting on top, near the handle. Of course, I snatched it, hoping the owner wouldn't see me and cause a scene. Before I knew it, I had reached into my purse, slipped on my shades, headed out the door, and pulled the large-brim hat as far down on my face as possible.

Outside, I jetted across the parking lot, realizing the weather was changing in Rochester. It was windy and was starting to get much cooler in the evenings. The darkness was perfect, making it harder to make out my disguise, but the wind kept hitting me in the face.

After making it to the car, my heart rate settled a bit. I dove into the front seat and backed out of the space doing thirty miles an hour. The police were already after me, so of course, I barged through the yellow gate where I was supposed to pay a fee. *Fuck rules,* I told myself. I was ready to go hard again, getting back to what I knew best.

It didn't take long to negotiate curve after curve, and I made it off the airport grounds safely, but now I had to make myself unnoticeable while I grabbed the children from the hotel. I was sure that by now everyone had seen my face splattered across their television screen. Yet I had to make things work.

Everything was happening so fast, I could barely think straight. I knew I had to get to the hotel, so I took the downtown exit and headed that way. Still, I worried about Oshyn. I hoped she was still alive so that I would have the opportunity to kill her myself. I wanted to live with the memory of being the person who took her life. Hers and her kids'.

Just then it hit me. My plan was coming together. Once at the hotel, I would kidnap the kids, put them in my trunk, and take them both to die with their mother. It would be sweet. *A family that dies together . . . how nice the sound.* I laughed.

Just as more crazy thoughts and anger filled my bones, flashing lights ahead made my heart stop momentarily. Sweat beaded against my forehead, and my wide brim hat began to itch my face. The six visible police cars and the five-car backup confirmed that my assumption was right. It was a roadblock. One I would have to pass.

"Fuck!" I shouted, thrusting my head down and banging it against the steering wheel.

I was the now the fourth car in line, and was breathing like an asthmatic. Fear filled my senses as I contemplated what I would say. It became clear that they were asking for identification by the way the officer talked nicely to the woman three cars ahead of me as she handed him something through her window. My guess . . . a driver's license.

"What fucking luck," I told myself while holding the wheel tightly, like my life depended on it. "A fugitive and a roadblock!"

Within seconds, we had moved up again, making me third in line. My heart beat even faster, and I decided to act as though my license had been lost once I got up to the officer in charge. I pumped myself up, believing everything would be okay, as I watched three officers rearing back on the hood of one of the cruisers. They laughed and grinned, as if they didn't have a care in the world. So my senses told me the roadblock had nothing to do with me. I had gotten sidetracked for a few moments after looking at the other officers' mannerisms. My nosiness cost me, though. Before I knew it, the man in front of me was asked to remove himself from his car.

Instantly, I panicked, backed up like a race car driver, and smashed into the white Camry behind me. It didn't take long before two of the laughing officers finally noticed me. Moments later, I made a U-turn after struggling to maneuver the steering wheel quickly enough. Before I knew it, I was racing down the wrong side of the road, with two police cars and blaring sirens behind me.

It was like the scene from the movie *Set It Off* where Queen Latifah refused to give in. I knew I wouldn't pull over. It wasn't my time for jail.

Had children to kidnap.

People to kill.

My destiny wasn't over.

27

Chloe

"Hello. My name is Oshyn Rodriquez," I said calmly, with a plastic smile spread across my face. "I misplaced my room key. Can I get another?"

My hands were folded neatly across one another as I leaned my body over the counter. I kept my smile going as the woman punched a few keys on the computer.

"What room number is that? I don't see Oshyn Rodriquez," the woman said.

Shit! I punched myself in the forehead for forgetting that Oshyn was married. "I mean Oshyn Jones," I corrected.

The woman looked at me strangely, then typed some more. I could tell she was going to be a problem from the way she refused to give me eye contact. She was a hater, a big-boned bitch who hated shapely women, but who shocked me with her next comment.

"Can I see some identification?"

"Look-a-here, Michelle," I said, eyeing her name tag, "I've had a long day. I lost my purse and then, to top it off, got pulled over by the cops." My voice started trembling as I switched into actress mode. "And . . . and . . . and . . . my daughter is sick, I mean really ill, and her father left me!" I started crying, tears dripping on the front desk, the whole nine. It went on for minutes, until I finally looked up to see Michelle's expression.

It was blank.

She wasn't feeling me.

At all.

Within seconds, I sniffed my fake snot back up into my nostrils and put my game face on. I knew nothing in life was free, so I pulled a twenty from my back pocket and laid it near her fingertips. From the looks of things, the chick shopped at T.J.Maxx, so a twenty was perfect. My first impulse was to reach over the counter and yank the bitch by the neck. But I chilled. I exhaled a few times, then spoke through my clenched teeth. "I need the key to my room please."

"Miss, I'll need to see some identification," she repeated, throwing the twenty back across the counter.

I got angry, reached across the counter, and

turned the black computer in my direction. "Cut the key," I told her in a fury.

She looked to her left, like she was signaling for backup. Little did she know, the name Brooklyn Jones, Room 254, was clearly exposed on the screen. Without delay, I slid back off my tiptoes and apologized mildly.

"Look, I've had a bad day. Forget about the key," I said politely. "I'll just wait over there for my husband." I grinned.

Michelle walked to the back without even saying another word. Maybe she was going to snitch, after all. I didn't care. It was about me and my mission. While I had the chance, I sped around the corner and dipped inside the breakfast area until Michelle was back in sight. She had talked about me for sure to a male employee, who showed up as backup. At one point they turned away, giving me my chance. I moved like an agent on a mission, making my way toward the stairwell. As soon as the coast was clear, I darted beneath the exit sign, opened the stairwell door, and ran up the staircase, headed to end the Jones name once and for all.

Taking two steps at a time, I wondered how I would get into the room. Bella was smart for her age, so letting me in was a no-no. I would have to be creative, sneaky, and pry my way in if necessary. Someone seeing me posed a big problem. The hotel wasn't packed at all, but nothing was ever safe when it came to killing.

When I reached the second floor, the feeling shook me a bit. It was sorta eerie and deserted, almost like nobody moved about frequently. I guess that was a good thing, since they wouldn't hear Bella scream. I didn't trust the bitch, Michelle, from the front desk. She might be on a mission to check the floor, just to see if I had doubled back. Then again, she didn't appear to be that smart.

Once on the floor, I moved slowly, checking for even numbers. Room 254 was just five doors down from the stairwell, and a sight for sore eyes. I wasted no time.

Boom, boom, boom! I banged on the door like the fuckin' police.

"Bella, open the door. It's Auntie." I laughed, then grabbed my stomach abruptly. I had been hit with a sudden pain, one deep inside my gut. "C'mon out, Bella!" I yelled. "You're not getting outta here alive," I sang.

Still nothing.

So I kicked the damn door.

"Bella, do you fuckin' hear me!"

I kicked it again, again and again, before stepping back. I decided to walk away, as if I were leaving. *Maybe she will be dumb enough to think I left, then open up,* I told myself. Just like that my feet trod slowly, moving backward past rooms 252, 250, and 248. Suddenly I stopped.

"Chloe!" someone called out.

"Oh shit!" Someone called my name. The voice I knew so well.

I turned around, exposing my victory grin when I saw her. I wanted to make her think I had already succeeded, had beaten her to the kids. Oshyn looked tired, worn, her hair in disarray. Probably needed a bath. She reminded me of Jason from *Friday the 13th* ... never wanting to die. How the fuck did she get loose? I asked myself.

"What did you do to my kids, Chloe?" She gritted her teeth and balled her fist in anger. Maybe her fiery stare was supposed to scare me. Maybe she wanted me to scream. Maybe the tone of her voice scared others, but not me.

Once again the pain hit me hard. A pain that damn near knocked me off my feet, but I stood up straight and stepped a few more feet away from the door. "Oh, we had a great time. I just left them inside," I teased. "They've gone to hell now," I boasted. "You'll see them both soon, bloody and all."

"Nooooooo, Chloe! Tell me you didn't!" she cried out, hurling her head into her hands.

I clutched my stomach, barely able to make it down the hallway, back in Oshyn's direction. It was a must that she died, and I had something I wanted to confess. But the intense cramping kept getting worse as I walked toward her, and she toward me. Just as fast, it started to feel like my intestines were being tied into tiny knots, but I kept talking shit.

"This is it, Oshyn. Your crazy ass gotta go." I wasn't sure how I would kill her, but I knew I would. She was coming at me full force with confidence, and for some strange reason, I thought she had a weapon in her hand. I stumbled, almost needing a cane, yet continued to walk her way. Before I could say something slick, I threw up. It was a smell that instantly stunk up the hallway, causing me to want to vomit again. Oshyn shrieked at the smell, which stopped her in her tracks. Then, out of nowhere, shit got worse. I became hot, my body like a furnace and my cheeks red like fire. Reality hit, and I was all of a sudden afraid of Oshyn.

Just four feet away she exposed the small blade, letting me know she was serious. For the first time in my life, Oshyn now had me afraid. I was so nauseous, I wasn't sure I could fight back.

Before I knew it, she had swung her foot around like she was on some Bruce Lee shit and had kicked me straight in the middle of my forehead. Instantly, I fell to the floor like a rag doll, then was immediately hit in the mouth with a powerful punch. Everything was happening so fast, I was unable to think, so I lay still, unsure if I could even move. Then, from the corner of my eye, I spotted a young man opening his door, peeping to see what all the commotion was about. I bellowed for help, but just like most black people, he wasn't trying to help. Within seconds he disappeared, and no one else came into view.

Vivid pictures of the gypsy's wrinkled face invaded my mind as I struggled to forget the red dust she'd blown in my face. Red dust that carried promises of wealth, true love, and revenge at the hands of another. So far, none of her predictions had come true. But the revenge piece now had possibilities.

Oshyn had begun throwing quick, powerful haymakers my way, proving that she had lost her mind. She hit me like Tyson banged out his opponents who never had the opportunity to fight back. She was whipping my ass, and there was nothing I could do about it. I was balled up in a knot and could only feel the whipping she was putting on my face and body. My vision had become blurry, and only the gypsy's face flashed before me as my body got weaker by the minute. My skin began to crawl with imaginary insects that I couldn't see or kill. I just lay on the floor, attempting to shield my head from my sister's vicious blows.

Nothing worked.

I just couldn't fight off the brutal beating.

"My children! Where are they, and what the fuck have you done with them!" Oshyn shouted as she hovered over me, desperately hoping for an answer.

I couldn't speak, could barely see. All I

wanted was a doctor or someone to help me. It wasn't just the pain from Oshyn's victory. My agony also stemmed from some sort of un-explainable illness taking over my body. It felt like an alien had entered my body. Blood dripped down the top of my head as I tried to raise it to talk to Oshyn.

Instead, I laughed when I looked at her face. "Ha-ha-ha-ha-ha-ha, you stupid bitch."

She snatched me by my neck like I was a rag doll. "Where are they?" she asked again and followed it up immediately with another blow to my face. This time with her fist, followed by a swipe across my forehead with the knife.

I stretched my jaw out in pain at just about the same time that I let out an agonizing sound. "Ahhhhh shit!" I wondered where she had gotten her energy from. I had tortured her days before and stolen her hope, yet she seemed invincible, and stronger than before.

"Where are they, Chloe?" she said, throwing another hard punch to my left jaw.

"Those muthafuckers are dead," I strug-gled to say, then smiled, showing all the blood that had stained my teeth and gums. "I chopped those bastards into pieces. Very . . . small . . . pieces," I told her, losing more en-ergy.

I expected her to cry, just like she did when she lost her first son. But she didn't. Strangely, the bitch grinned satanically and exhibited a sudden calmness. Oshyn pulled her right hand from her side, stared at the knife, and before I got a chance to say anything else, stabbed me in the abdomen.

"You . . . you . . . you . . . fucking . . . bitch . . . bitch!' I said in between my small, painful breaths. It was clear I now looked like a fish out of water, gulping for air. Praying for life. "You . . . you . . . stabbed me? *You* stabbed *me!*" I cried, wanting my voice to get louder.

I was dumbfounded.

Losing my fight.

Beat by Oshyn?

It wasn't supposed to end like this. She wasn't supposed to escape and grow some balls. I was supposed to win, I kept telling myself. I kept thinking about her weaknesses as she rammed the knife into my chest and stomach multiple times and kept it there as my life poured all over her. She had become a monster, someone I didn't know anymore. And as crazy as it sounded, my blood was now on her hands. All of it. All five pints that soiled my clothes and the carpet on the floor. And my death would soon follow.

"I loved you," Oshyn confessed as she dropped the weapon and stepped over me slowly. She cried like a punk, while her chest heaved up and down quickly. She wanted to say more, but I knew she wanted to get to the room to check on her kids.

I wanted to think about how I would've killed Bella if I had gotten in the room, but my eyes had begun their decent toward the back of my head, while my body temperature dropped drastically. I was cold, incoherent, but I still heard Oshyn's soft voice repeating, "I loved you."

She repeated more words as the tears streamed down her face, and she banged on her hotel door. Her fist beat the door rapidly and vigorously as she shouted her children's names.

"Bella, Mye," she screamed.

I knew she was probably still screaming, but I could no longer hear her. The floor had speedily been bombarded with employees and hotel guests rambling about in a panic, asking, "What happened!"

They were frantic as one woman kneeled to help me and another rushed to catch Oshyn. An employee opened Oshyn's door and announced that the room was empty.

I saw her mouth the words, "Where are my fucking kids!" just before her body dropped.

Weak bitch, I thought.

If only I had the energy to laugh.

The ability to tease.

The strength to take credit for their absence.

But I couldn't. I couldn't feel nothing anymore. Couldn't taste nothing, either. And could no longer see. My image of Oshyn lying back in someone's arms faded and was replaced with the gypsy. I was sure my spirit was slipping into death, as the old woman smiled

at me. Her lips were still crusty as she spoke
evil words.

Familiar words.

Words that had come true.

You will die . . . and burn in hell forever.

Within seconds everything was black.

28

Oshyn

"Bella!" I yelled. "Bella!"

I burst into the room after regaining consciousness. The bathroom was first. Then I checked under the beds and looked in the closet, right before peeking out at the patio. I didn't see anyone. Mye's bottles lay empty on the floor, and the bed was rumpled and undone.

"Bella, where are you!"

My cries fell on no one.

I flopped on the bed and buried my face in the messy white sheets, smearing Chloe's blood everywhere, while trying to cry my pain away. *Where could they be?* I asked myself, too emotionally and physically drained to actually come up with an answer. Maybe Chloe was telling the truth, I thought as more images of their little limbs being torn from their bodies filled my mind.

"Ju did good," a familiar voice behind me said. I popped my head up and spun around, only to see my grandmother standing in front of me, alone. "I am so proud of ju. Chloe was evil like her mother and a shame to our family. What ju did needed to be done," she assured me.

"Where are the kids?" I asked her.

"But this time she won't come back!" she said, totally ignoring my question. "Ju got rid of her for good. She's gone forever. Ju did good, my child."

"But where are Mye and Bella?"

"Now it's up to ju to build this family back up again. A strong bloodline of strong children."

"Why are you ignoring me?" I asked as I went to touch her shoulder, but my hand went right through her. I saw her, but she wasn't there. "Mama, please don't do this to me!" I screamed, but she just continued to talk over me. As if she wasn't responsible for the kids. As if I hadn't left them in her care. As if she didn't know who they were. "Don't do this to me!" I repeated one last time before the room began to spin.

"It's time for me to go, but I will always be in your presence. Watching over ju."

"But you were supposed to be watching over the kids!" I reminded her. "Where are they? Just don't leave! Please, tell me something before you go!"

She smiled and just simply repeated, "I will always be in your presence." And with that she was gone without a trace.

"Nooooo!" I yelled out in agony, but it was too late. I had been abandoned yet again. Feeling my knees getting ready to go out, I quickly sought refuge on the bed, where I lay down and curled up into a fetal position.

The room continued to spin as I tried coming to terms with Brooklyn and the kids being taken, but no amount of rocking could soothe the pain of loss I had in my chest. My heart no longer existed. In its place lay a shadow of darkness that was incapable of loving again. Not able to take the pain anymore, I took the bloody knife out of my pocket and for a moment just held it in my hand.

Chloe's blood stained the sheets I lay on, and now I was contemplating letting my own blood do the same. I would never feel Brooklyn's warm body and soft lips touch me again, and I would never hear the laughter of my baby or see Bella's green eyes look at me like a daughter would her mother. I'd been left on this earth to fend for myself, and I had made the decision to move on.

I held my left hand out and ran the razor-sharp blade across my wrists. I wanted my life to slip away quickly so I could join everybody sooner. The blood gushed out of my veins, and I felt my body getting weaker and weaker as my soul drifted away. A smile managed to make its way onto my face, and I closed my eyes to get ready for my journey to the light. Life as I knew it seemed to get a little colder.

My breathing slowed down.

Drastically.

And then it stopped.

29

Chloe

Three weeks later . . .

Miserable.
Still sick to the stomach.
And now frustrated.

It had been three weeks since my alterca-
tion with Oshyn, and only one week since my
release from Highland Hospital. Oshyn did
me in with her punk-ass stabbing, but I got
fixed. Crazy thing was that I still felt that shit
deep inside. My body lacked oomph, and my
stomach was beyond damaged.

Finally, I gathered enough energy to drag
myself into this whack-ass doctor's office,
where I now sat in the tiny waiting room, waiting. I decided to pull the *Today's Entrepreneur*
magazine from my purse to pass the time,
since it had been over two hours since the

doctor had first seen me, then sent me out to wait again.

Of course, he'd gone through his series of medical questions. Wanted to know my family history. I told him I had no family. Was left in the world all alone. Dr. Edwards shot me a sympathetic smile before continuing to ask about my symptoms. I told him how many days I'd had a fever, and how I had been nauseous off and on for the past few days. Once again, he shot me a pitiful look.

"You may be pregnant," I remembered him saying casually. "Would that be a good thing for you or bad?"

His comments were unethical, but I knew it was hard for him to remain professional by the way he studied me. He really wanted to know if I had a man. Was I committed was what he wanted to ask. And he definitely wanted me. I could feel it. He had been flirting with me from the moment I walked into his examination room.

"I'm not seeing anybody seriously, but I've had a relationship or two," I stated.

"Is that so?" he commented, moving closer. "You have a steady boyfriend?"

"Nope, but the job is open." I opened my legs wide, hoping he could see my pussy hairs beneath the white paper robe he'd given me.

"We'll see about that." He grinned widely, showing every tooth in his mouth. "My goodness, Chloe, where did you get all those scratches and bruises on the side of your face? And your neck," he added, clutching my chin.

"Rough sex," I teased. "Doc, I think there's a lump on my breast. Can you check it for me?"

"Chloe, that might not be a good idea in here. There's another time, another place for that." He stopped to watch me fondle my breast. "But this is the time to say, protect yourself in the future," he preached, before telling me I would have to take a pregnancy test, two other tests, and get my blood checked for a rare disease. He said the nurse would come in to do everything.

I just remembered nodding to everything he said, considering that he had me hypnotized. Everyone in the office had noticed, too, I was sure.

Truth be told, the nigga was fine, so he could shoot me as many personal and affectionate looks as he wanted. He was in his midthirties, was lighter than I liked my men, but had a nice body, and a hell of a practice. I could see myself with him, as long as he made me a kept woman, and in charge of the bitches at the front desk. I was tired of the chasing-money scene and had thought about going after a professional man with big money. Legal money.

I knew Dr. Edwards's office made crazy money by the number of patients he had, and the fact that we all waited for hours due to the number of people being seen in the office. I snapped back to the present and got pissed when I saw him walk past the front office, where he laughed along with the head nurse with a thousand micro-braids, whom I hated with a passion.

His eyes darted over in my direction, and he said, "Just a few more minutes, Chloe."

I nodded, then added an evil smirk just before zooming in on Tommy's article.

"Just waiting for the results of the last test."

My arms were crossed, and my body was slumped down in the chair. "No problem, Doc," I said. "Did you just want me to be last so we can be alone?" I added sarcastically.

He knew I was referring to the fact that there were now only two people left in the waiting room with me. But he took my comment in stride. "No, it's not that. We sent your blood down to the lab for testing. We called down, and they said they are reviewing the other two tests you took."

I started thinking about the possibility of me being pregnant. The possibility of carrying someone inside of me, then raising the child I would call my own. *Damn, that's what my mother did, and she fucked my life up!* I thought, stomping the floor.

I wasn't ready. I knew it. I wasn't like Oshyn, who was the type of person who wanted to make breakfast every morning, comb hair, check homework, and do all the other bull-shit that went along with being a mother. I wanted to be a hooker and a housewife all in the same breath.

The thought of Oshyn sent my mind wandering. It was to a place that was pleasant for me. The graveyard. The place where all my folk roamed. Word on the street was that Oshyn was really dead. Dead as in six feet under. Streets said she did it to herself at the hotel when she thought she had me. I would've given anything to see it. And killed her a second time if given the chance.

The craziest part of it all was that there was no funeral. I searched high and low, trying to get information about the location of her body, hopefully, so I'd have one more chance to get at Bella. The latest reports told me somebody had Oshyn's body shipped to an unknown location to be buried. I wondered who. And why. *We* had no family. *We* had no friends. And she no longer had Brooklyn.

Then my thoughts switched back to Tommy and the magazine I held in my hand. I started reading the feature article and realized just after two minutes of reading that Tommy had really been getting money. It talked about how he was living the good life, while battling health challenges, and was missing love in his life. It said he was looking for someone to love, and to share his life and fortune with.

I got angry.

Threw the magazine across the floor.

Decided I would get up and stomp on it.

But suddenly I was interrupted.

"Ahhh . . . Ms. Rodriquez, you can come on back," the nurse said.

"Finally," I mumbled, rushing from the waiting area around to where the nurse stood. She had a pencil stuck in between her braids and was scratching for dear life.

"Follow me."

"Took you long enough," I belted.

She stopped in the middle of the narrow hallway, causing my body to bump into hers. Turning slowly, she threw her hands on her hips, ready to blast me. "It took a while because the lab workers wanted to double-check your results." She spat her words out slowly, and the look on her face was grim.

After watching her expression, I decided to shut up and just followed her into the room. I could tell she was mad as she pulled a new white covering onto the table, instructing me to leave my clothes on this time. She never gave me eye contact, simply gave off a weird vibe.

"The doctor should be in shortly," she said, slamming the door behind her.

"Fuck that bitch," I belted while staring at the blank white walls around me. I hopped up on the table, thinking about the outcome of my pregnancy. And thinking about how I would fuck Edwards before we left the room. My bitch-ass nurse had told me not to get undressed, but I considered doing it, anyway. I was wondering what Doc Edwards would say if he walked in and saw me ass naked on his examining table. I laughed to myself, trying to get happy, because I figured my news wasn't so great.

I had already come to grips with the fact that I was pregnant. I didn't think I could conceive after how Oshyn tore my insides out with that blade. The stabbing was treacherous, but I had been through worse. Two weeks in the hospital was it. I was tough like that. Like Michelin tires, built to last. So if I was pregnant, I had two choices: hop up on somebody's table and have them vacuum my womb or become a mother. If I chose the latter, the plan was to get knocked up this month by some paid-ass dude, then tell him that the baby was his. I laughed again, until I heard the three knocks on the door.

"C'mon in," I said seductively, then threw my right leg over the left.

"Chloe," the doc said, peeping before opening the door all the way.

I sat up straight. "I'm ready to hear. What's up?"

"Soooo," he began uneasily.

Quickly, I changed my mood, because his

was so damn depressing. He'd done a complete three-sixty from the Mr. Bubbly he had portrayed just an hour ago.

"Doc, it can't be that bad. If I'm pregnant, we can still be together."

I laughed. He didn't.

"Hey, I was thinking maybe we could get together tonight." I waited. And waited, hoping for a response. "It's okay," I said, clutching my stomach. "I know you're feeling me, and I'm definitely feeling you. The daddy is long gone."

Doc Edwards pushed his palm toward my face, signaling me to stop. Every sign of joy had been removed from his face.

"Doc, give it to me straight, no chaser."

"Chloe, I sent your blood work down to the lab. You agreed to get tested for HIV, although that's not what I thought you had . . . but your test results are positive."

I fell back onto the table, attempting to catch my breath. "Did you say *positive?* As in I got HIV?"

I started breathing hard.

Fast.

Uncontrollably.

"Calm down, Chloe." The doctor took two steps in my direction.

"Calm down? That shit that kills people!" I blurted out. It seemed like my body overheated in just seconds, causing me to pull my hair back for some relief.

"Chloe, understand that you are in the early

stages of HIV. You do not have AIDS." He paused, allowing his brows to crinkle. "Not yet, anyway."

"Fuck . . . fuck . . . fuck!" I shouted, then threw my head back in anguish.

His whole demeanor had changed. His tone wasn't as friendly, and he damn sure wasn't interested in flirting anymore. I watched him closely as he stood three steps away from me, writing several notes on my chart. I wanted to ask questions but was still partially in a state of shock.

"What does this mean?" I snarled, attempting to regain my composure.

A knock sounded at the door; then it opened slowly. The person I didn't want to see stood there with several pamphlets and a clipboard.

"Chloe, my head nurse, Shaniqua, will take it from here. I've got an appointment."

Shaniqua stood in the doorway, unsympathetically waiting for Doctor Edwards to slip behind her. No sooner had he left than she started in on me.

"Okay, not sure if you know, but one of the main causes of HIV is through sexual intercourse. It can enter your body through certain membranes of the anus, vagina, or mouth. So, I'm sure you know how you got it." She paused and ran her long fingernail up and down the list on her paper. "Question is . . . can you get in touch with all your recent sexual partners to notify them?"

The entire time Shaniqua talked, my eyes remained glassy. At one point I could see her lips moving but heard nothing. My life had taken a turn that I never expected.

"HIV," I said to myself slowly.

"Do you hear me, Ms. Rodriquez!"

"Bitch, I hear you!" I shouted back.

The nurse from hell popped her neck backward, wanting to get hood with me. She must've thought about her job and decided to continue reading from the paper. "Okay, on to the meds. They are pricey, so get ready to spend."

I just sat still, staring off into space.

"There's a wide range to choose from. Emtriva costs roughly three hundred fifty dollars a month, and then there's Fuzeon. That'll run you about twenty-five hundred dollars a month."

"Are you done?" I asked, lifting myself off the table. I showed no emotion.

"Listen, Ms. Rodriquez, this is not a death sentence," she said, sounding as if she cared for the first time. "You just have to take the medication and learn to live with it."

"Yeah. Sure. This is great."

"Listen, this is important," she said to me, after seeing my hand on the doorknob. "Make sure you wear a condom so that you don't infect others."

I laughed heartily, as if I hadn't just gotten word that I had HIV. I opened the door confidently, telling myself I would get through this. Like I did in every other aspect of my life. I would use this situation to come out on top. No matter what others would say, I would make it work for me.

Then it hit me as I walked back down the narrow hallway. I didn't have to lose my mistress status because of some nagging-ass disease. I laughed heartily. "It won't take control of me," I boasted. "I will take control of it." And every nigga who came in contact with me would get infected. If they paid me well, they could possibly get the memo in a decent amount of time to get treated. Others . . . well, fuck 'em. They'd get what they deserved.

I stopped by the front desk on my way out, only to see Dr. Edwards behind the computer table, snuggled up with a nurse. It didn't bother me. He was fair game.

"Hey, Doc, you sure you don't want to go out tonight?" I stuck my tongue out for added effect. Of course, he turned his head. But I walked out of his office as if nothing had changed. Not my attitude, and not my ruthless intentions in life. But, indeed, my whole life had changed.

Had places to go.

People to fuck.

And niggas to infect.

30

Oshyn

This was it.

Death.

My spirit effortlessly lifted from my body and floated to the illuminating light that awaited me. It seemed as though my eyes had become immune to the light, which had once blinded me, as I didn't have to shield them for protection. This time, I was *supposed* to be here. I looked down at my body, which was covered in blood, and was instantly saddened that it all had to end like this.

So tragic.

So alone.

So painfully.

But I was tired of all that life had to offer me, and was ready for it all to be over. My whole family had now crossed over to the other side, and I wanted to be with them. This was the only choice I had.

"Mommy!" Micah screamed as he ran to me. His long and hard embrace let me know that he wasn't mad about me leaving him before, just happy I had returned, as promised.

I dug my head in his shoulder and whispered, "I'll never leave you again!"

When I lifted my head back up, I saw that my mother, Roslyn, my grandmother, and Apples had all gathered around and were waiting patiently for their chance to greet me. We had eternity. There was no rush. My best friend, Apples, hadn't changed one bit. Long, curly locks, a freckled face, and green eyes were still permanent fixtures, and her immortality seemed to have made her even more beautiful than before.

"Thank you for taking care of Bella," she said to me as we hugged. "I watched you the whole time, and I'm grateful that you took her in and loved her like your own."

"But we're family, and you would've done the same for me," I said right before I looked over at Micah. "As a matter of fact, you did do that for me!"

"Welcome home, baby!" My mother, who had been taken out of my life at the hands of Chloe, was now here with me. We hugged and kissed, cherishing the fact that we were all back together again.

"Where's Mahogany?" I asked.

"She's with Chloe," my mother answered back. I was hoping that I'd see the two of them together, happy again, but I was sure that Chloe needed her mother more.

"Where is my husband? The kids?" I asked everyone as I looked around.

"What are you talking about?" my mother answered. "There not here."

"But they're supposed to be! Where are they?"

"No, take a look."

My mother pointed down and redirected my attention back to my hotel room. Back to my dead body. Just as I was about to tell her that I didn't see anything, the door opened and Bella walked in, followed by Brooklyn, with our son in one hand and his other hand in a sling. And then they screamed.

I looked on in horror as Brooklyn handed Mye off to Bella and ran over to my cold body to check for a pulse. Then he screamed out my name and, like the pulse confirmed, got no answer.

"He was dead! Brooklyn was murdered! I saw it with my own eyes. He was shot and then died!" I insisted.

"No. The bullet hit his arm. Main artery. Paramedics came and saved his life before he bled out," my mother explained.

"They are still alive," I screamed to my grandmother. "Why didn't you just tell me that they were still alive?"

She never answered my question, just looked away.

"Take me back!" I screamed, no longer wanting to be here. "Take me back!"

"There is no going back, sweetheart. This is where your home is now." My mother grabbed my hand and attempted to pull me closer toward the light. "Don't fight it," she said, noticing my resistance. "This was a choice that you made."

"But I thought that they were here! Let me go!"

But she didn't.

The visual of them crying over my body slowly faded away as I was forced closer to the light. This was now my future, and the past had to be left behind.

Don't miss Tiphani Montgomery's

The Millionaire Mistress

On sale now from Dafina Books

1

Oshyn

2001

"Where the fuck have you been?" I asked Trent, smelling his funky weed from across the room.

He immediately ducked from the cordless phone that was flying straight toward his head. It only missed because of my swollen eyes. I had been crying the ugly cry.

"Bitch, don't question me. Your young ass needs to play your position, and be lucky I'm still taking care of you!"

"Oh, so now I'm a young bitch? I'm eighteen years old and eight months pregnant with your son and I'm a bitch? Two fucking days, Trent! You been gone for two fucking days, and you couldn't even call to let me know that you were okay?" I stood with my hands below my protruding belly, ready to slice his ass. "You come walking in here at nine o'clock in the morning after being missing in action, and I'm a bitch? When did it get like this? What did I do to deserve being treated like shit?" I asked, crying like a little baby. I promised myself I wouldn't get soft, at least not this time. I couldn't help it, though; my feelings were torn apart. "When did you stop loving me?" I screamed.

Silence.

Dead silence.

I stared at the man who used to love me. The man whose six-two frame used to smother me with hugs after a long day of getting money. The man who loved to sit between my legs and kiss my thighs while I braided his long, thick hair. I looked at the gold fronts on the bottom of his teeth, which enhanced his already perfect smile, remembering how sexy he used to make me feel. Trent looked a little different now—same body, different soul.

I wished I had a sixth sense so I could figure out exactly what was wrong with him. Him staying out all night was becoming all too familiar. I guess in a way part of me was in denial. I watched him ignore me as I stared off into space. *Maybe reminiscing about the past will bring back some good memories*, I thought.

It's funny how your life turns out, because I didn't like Trent when we first met two years ago. We were at Rush-Henrietta High School's basketball tournament. He was a twenty-year-old, well-known dope boy and stick-up kid, known for having money and a flashy lifestyle, but I wasn't impressed. Most of the people I hung around were guys, and I knew about all the games they played with the countless bitches they chased. None of my homeboys were worth shit, and they didn't want anything more than some pussy or head from whatever groupie was willing to give it to them.

To me, Trent wasn't different, but he was annoyingly persistent. He had a little dough, and word on the street was that he snatched up any chick that crossed his path. It was out of character for him to have someone like me brushing him off. He was used to bitches dropping their panties at the drop of a dime, but not me. I wasn't interested in being added to the "I fucked her" club.

He was persistent as hell. I remember days when Trent would wait for me at my bus stop with dozens of red roses and fluffy teddy bears. At first, I was hesitant, but eventually I accepted the roses, stuffed animals, and the other gifts that followed.

"Why don't you just leave me alone?" I finally asked one day, aggravated at his constant uninvited presence. To the onlookers, he was just a sweet guy trying to treat me nice, but I knew the truth; boys were all the same. He wanted something in return for all the gifts he'd gotten me, and it was most likely pussy. I was one of the few virgins left in my school, and I wasn't going to ruin my reputation by giving up some ass.

Trent begged to take me out, promising that if I didn't enjoy myself he would leave me alone for good. That was an offer too good to refuse, so I agreed to the one date, and since then we were inseparable. Not once did he try to fuck or disrespect me in any way. It wasn't until a few months later that I decided to give him what I cherished the most, my virginity.

Sex with Trent was everything a girl could imagine. His gentle touch and delicate stroke had me hooked. He knew exactly how to make me feel good and I loved every minute of it. I guess that's why after I found out about my pregnancy, my excitement was uncontrollable. I knew at that point I had him for life.

While we were pillow talking one night, Trent told me that he knocked me up on purpose. Surprisingly to him, I didn't get upset. The smile on my face widened and I jumped into his arms without hesitation. The fact that we would be a family had me happier than a faggot with a dick in his mouth.

On occasions, he would always tell me how much he cared for me, and that he wanted me to have his son, be his wife, and raise his family. I believed him and had no doubt that he'd be a good father to his children. Trent vowed to raise our kids better than his crack-head parents. He had five sisters and one brother, all younger and still living in the foster care system. He hated his mother for that. Maybe that's why he insisted on serving her when the monkey on her back came scratching.

I asked him once why he insisted on giving his mother the drugs. That was after I watched her deteriorating body thank him for the poison that ran through her veins daily. I told him that he needed to help her. My suggestion was to admit her into rehab and not condone her habit any longer. I tried putting myself in his shoes, but just couldn't see doing that to my mother.

Trent snapped, with a little hostility in his voice, saying that he would rather give drugs to her for free than to wonder which one of his homeboys she fucked or sucked to get her fix. He also made it clear to never question him again about his mother. I left the subject alone, still feeling crazy about the whole idea of him serving his mother, but I realized that his back was against the wall with very few options. Deep down inside, I think he wanted to be responsible for her slow death.

When we talked about the pregnancy, Trent informed me that Steve, his best friend, would be the godfather. Steve and Trent grew up together on the east side of Rochester, New York. They were closer than brothers, the only family each had ever known. When I was four months pregnant, Steve went missing. His girlfriend called Trent when he didn't come home from a run. Trent immediately knew something was seriously wrong. In Rochester, New York, hustling and coming up missing only meant one thing . . . death.

Trent searched and searched, and asked questions from Rochester to Harlem. Two months later, Steve's body was found decapitated inside of a plastic bag at the bottom of the Genesee River. Some said it was the mob, others said it was a stick-up gone wrong, but no matter what happened that night, Trent hadn't been right ever since.

His behavior mocked that of a person whose weed had been laced with angel dust. His mind was gone. Then the rumors came. It seemed this nigga just couldn't keep his dick in his pants. He was never satisfied. I ended up cutting a couple of bitches up over him. With my son in my stomach, I foolishly fought over dick that wasn't mine. Apparently never was.

I recalled a time when I was five months pregnant. I asked Trent if he wanted to go to the movies to get his mind off of Steve. He hadn't been social, and I wanted us to spend a little more time together. He brushed me off, saying that he was busy and needed to make a run. I was hurt as hell when he strutted out the door, leaving a trail of his old-ass Cool Water cologne behind. Things seemed suspicious, but I couldn't pinpoint anything.

I yelled as the door shut in my face, "Don't forget my food!"

That night I decided to stay in and take some time for myself. My cell phone rang a few times, but I ignored it. My instinct told me it was Trent so I decided to check the caller ID. I saw that it was my homegirl, Apples, so I quickly answered the phone.

Before I could say hello, she unloaded all the details of her spotting Trent and some light-skinned bitch that went to Franklin High School at the movies. She said everybody saw them hugged up and kissing all over each other. I was sick to my stomach! *I asked that motherfucker to go with me to the movies, and he's there with some bitch!* I could hear Apples hyperventilating through the phone. She acted as if Trent was her man. The next thing I knew, she told me to get ready, she was on the way to my house.

I hurried when her words, "If we hustle, we can catch them as they come out the theatre," registered.

I remember hanging up the phone, still shocked at what I had just heard. *But he was supposed to be on the way home with my Country Sweet Chicken,* I thought, wondering why he would do something like that to me. His actions explained a lot of things, though. Trent hadn't touched me in a while, and maybe a new woman was why. He had gotten another bitch and was slowly kicking me out of his life, but I wasn't going without a fight.

Apples pulled up to the crib, and we made

it back to the movies in record time. We cased the parking lot, making sure Trent's burgundy Tahoe was still there. We spotted his truck, parked in the cut, and watched like two detectives on a stakeout. I rubbed my hands nervously around my belly, wishing my baby could comfort me. An hour passed and there still was no sign of Trent or his bitch. I banged my fist on the dash.

"Damn, what the fuck did they go see?" I shouted.

Apples said nothing. She was ready for war. Just as she pulled out the Vaseline, we finally noticed a group of people walking out of the theater. I thought my eyes were deceiving me when I saw Trent with his arm wrapped around some chick's shoulders. He had a big smile on his face, something that I hadn't seen in a while.

I jumped out of the car like Rambo, and ran straight toward them. Not saying a word, I swung, cutting the bitch in the face with my box cutter. She didn't have any idea who I was, and she definitely didn't know what I'd cut her with. Trent was shocked. He looked like he wanted to run for help, but instead his eyes stayed glued on me. I'm not sure if it was because of all the blood that was squirting out of her face, or because he had been caught. Maybe it was a combination of both, but either way, the nigga quickly removed his arm as she fell to the ground holding her face.

Trent opened his mouth to justify himself, and before he could utter an explanation, I swung the blood-covered box cutter toward his face, barely missing it. Before I knew it, his punk ass was screaming like a bitch. His right hand had been split wide open, and I didn't give a fuck.

My young mind couldn't comprehend why any of that happened to me. I was a model girlfriend, didn't hang out, cooked, cleaned, and did my best to keep him satisfied. I even moved out of my Grandma's crib and in with him once I got pregnant.

Although Trent forgave me after the incident at the movies, our relationship was never the same. Just when I thought things would get better, Trent eventually started coming home later and sometimes not at all. I was tired of being treated like the other woman, and decided to stand my ground.

When I questioned him about his late hours, he'd get verbally abusive and threaten to leave me, but today was different. I didn't give a fuck what happened. I was sick of being treated like shit, sick of being neglected. *This can't be what love is about*, I reasoned with myself, thinking this wasn't the man I met two years ago. I was determined to put an end to his madness.

"Trent," I said, bringing myself back to reality. I had done so much reflecting that I forgot I'd asked him a question. "I asked you, when did you stop loving me?" I repeated, as if he hadn't heard me the first time.

Still no answer.

He made himself comfortable at the kitchen table, pretending to be busier than he really was, counting out the money scattered around the money machine.

"Where the fuck you been?" I screamed, frustrated that he was ignoring me. I knocked the neatly placed stacks of one-hundred-dollar bills off the table. The dirty money fluttered everywhere, hitting us in the face as it landed. There was a light scent of currency in the air that I hated. I didn't know if it was because of the pregnancy, but I could smell everything, especially dirty money.

"You stupid bitch!" Trent yelled.

I flinched from his deformed hand that was raised in the air, the hand that I marked for life. Trent had never hit me before, even when I stabbed him. I guess he realized what he was doing and put his hand back down.

"Stop asking me all these stupid ass questions, Oshyn," he said while walking away from the table. "Now have this shit picked up, some food on my table, and your pussy ready when I get out the shower!" he demanded.

So much for being hard, I thought to myself.

Thoughts of leaving Trent entered my mind, but I loved him. He was all I had ever known. He was my first, my last, my everything, as

Barry White would say. I thought this was how a relationship was supposed to go.

I put my long hair into a ponytail because it kept sticking to my tear-stained face. My round belly and weak heart didn't allow for easy bending, so I took my time picking up the mess I made when his cell phone rang. At that point, I was frustrated and definitely didn't want Trent to leave for a run. I was ready to hide the phone until I glanced at the caller ID.

"Hello?" I answered quickly, wanting to know who Chocolate was.

"Is this Oshyn?" she asked with a nasty attitude. I knew where this was headed. I'd had these conversations before—different bitch, same topic.

"Who the fuck is this?" I barked.

"This is Chocolate and I want to let you know that Trent is my man, and I'm pregnant with his baby, bitch, so you need to stop calling him in the middle of the night so that we can get some sleep!"

"Who the fuck you think you talking to? You can't know who I am!" I said, hitting her back with a question. Anyone who knew my MO wouldn't dare step to me with this bullshit, especially over this nigga. I'd kill a bitch over his dick. "Where you at, bitch? I'm coming to see you!"

"I'm at 521 North Clinton Avenue," she said, almost daring me to come.

This dumb broad actually lived on my side of town. "I'm on my way!" I shouted. After hanging up the phone, I considered asking Trent who Chocolate was, but chose not to, considering how our conversation just ended. Going to her crib was a must. I was too furious not to go. Besides, she probably had information that would satisfy some of my unanswered questions. I hated the thought of going out into the freezing cold, but this was crucial.

I threw on my black North Face coat, Timberlands and oversized mittens, and snuck out the crib. I ran up the street to the corner store and, just my luck, a cab was sitting there waiting for a fare. He took me to Chocolate's house, and I paid him a little extra to wait just in case something popped off.

I arrived at the spot, raced to the door, and started kicking it as hard as I could.

"Come out, bitch!" I screamed at the top of my lungs, hoping that she heard me. I kicked the door harder, leaving a slight dent on the aging wood. It finally opened.

She was short, struggling to even be five-two, and chunky. Her wavy red hair touched her wide waist and protruding stomach that confirmed her claim of being pregnant. The bitch was huge and her nose was quite scary. Yeah, she was pregnant for real.

"What's up now?" she asked, pointing her chubby fingers in my face.

That was the biggest mistake she could have ever made. I never talked, just swung. I spit out my razor like a professional blade slinger and slashed her face wide open from her eyebrow to her cheek. Chocolate's flesh split wide open and blood gushed everywhere. She fell to her knees on the wooden porch and screamed in agony while trying to hold her face together. No one heard us, and if they did, they didn't care. These were the sounds that we were used to in the hood, and it was music to everyone's ears compared to random gunshots.

I kicked her in the stomach multiple times with my Timbs, until I could barely breathe. I glanced behind me to make sure no one was watching. With all of my might, I turned around and hit her one last time.

"Don't call Trent's fucking phone again!" I demanded, still gasping for air. My chest heaved in and out heavily as I walked back to the cab.

I was back to the crib in less than twenty minutes flat. I barged in the house with my hand caressing my cramping stomach, screaming to the top of my lungs.

"Trent! Who the fuck is Chocolate . . . Treeennnt?"

"Shut the fuck up with all that screaming!" he said, walking from the bedroom to the front door. He paused and looked at me. His dark eyes examined my trembling body. He blurted out, like he was pissed at me, "Where the fuck have you been? Why you got blood all over you?"

"Oh, now you want to know where I've been! Don't question me, you bitch ass nigga, after you knocked another bitch up! Let's see if you can look in her sliced up face while you fuck her now, you bitch ass . . ." WHOP!

Trent rocked me in the face with his fist. He then walked into our bedroom, grabbed a handful of clothes, and threw them out the front door. I panicked, realizing the clothes belonged to me.

"Get the fuck out my house!" he yelled, with his fingers pointing to the dark street.

The door was wide open and I could feel the strong chill. "But where am I supposed to go?" I asked, turning my anger into tears. While I tasted the blood that trickled into my mouth, my heart sank. "What about our baby?"

"I don't even know if it's mine, bitch. Beat it!"

With that, he pushed me out the house and slammed the door. The thunderous sound of the door closing in my face echoed through my ears, making my headache much more painful.

It hurt so bad, I could barely breathe. Why would he even question the paternity of our child? I cried like a baby on the steps, scared to move. I couldn't understand why I was sitting outside our house, eight months pregnant, in December.

"AAAHHHHHHHHH!" I screamed, balled over in pain. The cramping in my stomach had gotten worse, and the thought of losing my baby had me terrified. "Trent, let me in! Something isn't right!" I screamed, holding my stomach tightly. With the little energy left in me, I pounded on the door like the police. Something was definitely wrong, because the pain was almost unbearable. "Trent, please help me," I said in between gasps for air.

The pain was hitting me once every few minutes, so I couldn't walk for help. I sat shivering on the front porch, waiting for Trent to come to his senses. I felt my stomach switch positions, no longer sitting high, where it once was.

"AAAAAHHHHH!" I wailed again, at the top of my lungs. The pain knocked me down to the ground, where I ended up stretched out in the snow. I just laid there, freezing. There was no way that I could move. The pain was absolutely paralyzing.

I blacked out.

I woke up on a stretcher, getting ready to be lifted into the ambulance. The red-haired female paramedic told me that my neighbor saw me laid out in the snow. He knew I was pregnant and called for help.

"Good thing he did," she said in her soft

nurturing voice. "Your water broke and your contractions are a minute apart." She took a moment and softly moved my frizzy hair out of my face. "We've checked your skin and there aren't any puncture wounds anywhere … whose blood is this? What happened? Is someone else hurt?"

I ignored the freckle-faced lady who was only there to help, and laid on the stretcher, feeling like I was near death. My body was numb, probably from being covered in the snow.

I stared at the house that was once my home and noticed Trent staring out our bedroom window. Our eyes met. I mouthed, "Why?"

He looked at me with a cold pair of eyes. I turned my head slightly, hoping that my eyes were deceiving me. I could've sworn he mouthed FUCK YOU. He closed the curtain and I never saw him again.

My introduction to love had left me for dead.